What the critics are saying...

Five Stars "Ms. Hamre has a creative and interesting storyline in this erotic romance... The sex is phenomenal and...truly done beautifully. This book will make a nice addition to your bedside table." ~ *Julie Esparza Just Erotic Romance Reviews*

Five Flames "Ms. Hamre writes a very unique BDSM love story, one of an undisciplined submissive and her dominant personal trainer...this novel is a treat that combines the perks of self-control and discipline with sexual pleasures and gratification. It is sensual, highly sexual, and ultimately pleasing." ~ *Ansley Fallen Angel reviews*

Five Coffee Cups "I found this book absorbing. It drew me right in and kept me there. I loved the by play of emotions between the two characters; from Norris refusing to comply with the way Adrian wanted her to submit to her feelings for him after he helps her accomplish her goal. This book is very much a keeper for me and I recommend it for those want to read about a Master and his submissive." ~ *Sheryl Coffee Time Romance*

D0972868

Four Slippers "The story contains really hot erotica, details of a developing D/s relationship, bondage and sexual practices some might find objectionable, but that is one of the very reasons why *Sweet Discipline* is not only a scorching read but also one that is riveting and entertaining. This is no vanilla fairy tale. You may guess by my name that I find the power exchange is more potent than a vanilla story any day. Definite kudos to *Bonnie Hamre,* and I am wishing her a long career at Ellora's Cave and waiting impatiently for her next release." ~ *Maitresse Novel Spot Romance Reviews*

Sweet DISCIPLINE

Bonnie Hamre

ELLORA'S CAVE
ROMANTICA PUBLISHING

An Ellora's Cave Romantica Publication

www.ellorascave.com

Sweet Discipline

ISBN # 1419952633
ALL RIGHTS RESERVED.
Sweet Discipline Copyright© 2004 Bonnie Hamre
Edited by: *Briana St. James*
Cover art by: *Lissa Waitley*

Electronic book Publication: August, 2004
Trade paperback Publication: October, 2005

Warning:

The following material contains graphic sexual content meant for mature readers. *Sweet Discipline* has been rated *E-rotic* by a minimum of three independent reviewers.

Ellora's Cave Publishing offers three levels of Romantica™ reading entertainment: S (S-ensuous), E (E-rotic), and X (X-treme).

S-*ensuous* love scenes are explicit and leave nothing to the imagination.

E-*rotic* love scenes are explicit, leave nothing to the imagination, and are high in volume per the overall word count. In addition, some E-rated titles might contain fantasy material that some readers find objectionable, such as bondage, submission, same sex encounters, forced seductions, etc. E-rated titles are the most graphic titles we carry; it is common, for instance, for an author to use words such as "fucking", "cock", "pussy", etc., within their work of literature.

X-*treme* titles differ from E-rated titles only in plot premise and storyline execution. Unlike E-rated titles, stories designated with the letter X tend to contain controversial subject matter not for the faint of heart.

Sweet Discipline

Chapter One

"All it takes is discipline."

Norris Brownell studied her friend Kendra who'd spoken so emphatically. Since she'd last had dinner with Kendra and her husband Paul, Kendra had dropped out of sight and reemerged looking svelte, chic and twenty-five pounds thinner. "I can't believe it," Norris said. "Between the two of us, we've tried every diet known to man, and then some."

Kendra's eyes sparkled. "Not *every* one."

"So tell me." Norris twirled spaghetti carbonara onto her fork as she leaned over the restaurant table. "How did you do it?"

"I can't tell you. I promised I wouldn't divulge any er…trade secrets."

"Not even a hint?" Norris coaxed though a glance at Kendra's salad of mixed greens and raw vegetables gave her a huge hint. Before Kendra's spa experience, they both would have been eating pasta, drinking wine and anticipating a slice of tiramisu.

Kendra glanced around, scoping out eavesdroppers. "It's not the usual diet program. It's demanding, tough and I cried a lot," she whispered. "But it was worth it."

"Whatever you had to do, you look fabulous." Kendra's skin looked soft and lustrous. Her eyes were clear and bright, shining with confidence. "How does Paul like your new look?"

"He adores it. He can't keep his hands off me." Kendra leaned closer. "And the sex is terrific! You wouldn't believe some of the things we've tried. I never dreamed sex could be so wild, so…" She rolled her eyes.

Norris got the point. In fact, her imagination could supply any number of fantasies. She was glad for Kendra, of course she was, but hearing hints about her friend's fantastic sex life wasn't easy. Not when she wasn't getting any. Not as much work as she wanted, either.

Very few people wanted to hire a consultant to advise them about management practices if she couldn't manage her own weight. When she'd branched out on her own and started her consulting practice, she'd worked such long hours, she'd had no thought for food. It hadn't been necessary to watch her weight, but as her practice grew, and she hired staff and associates, her schedule was less frantic and there were a satisfying number of successes to celebrate with wine and food. The pounds had crept back, so stealthily she hadn't noticed until her clients and associates started giving her disapproving looks. Business was still good, her long-time clients were loyal, but new ones were harder to attract. Her business wasn't growing. And she had ambitions, dreams and goals she wanted to make happen. She needed more work, big-name, prestigious clients, to make that next move up that slippery success ladder.

If she had to change herself to make that climb, then she would. Once she was slim and bolstered her willpower, she'd have no trouble convincing clients she could make their problems go away, too. And when she was slim and sexy, Jack Rodriguez would do more than nod when they met around a conference table. Eat your heart out, Jack.

"How can I get into it, too?" she asked eagerly. "What's it called?"

Kendra toyed with her salad. "It's not for everyone. They're discreet, they don't advertise and they don't take everyone. They're very strict and you've never liked anyone telling you what to do. I'm afraid you'll either quit or be asked to leave."

"To look like that," Norris gestured at her friend's sleek figure. "Add sex and I can take anything!"

"I don't know." Kendra looked dubious. "The first few days are very hard. I didn't think I could do it." She dipped her fork in her dressing, then shook most of it off before spearing an arugula leaf. "You won't be able to. You get ticked off at something and then—"

"C'mon, Kenny. I'm not that bad."

"Sure you are." She eyed Norris speculatively. "Look, you're my friend and I think the world of you. You've got a loving heart, but you're obstinate. It's a good thing you excel at what you do or your clients would go somewhere else." She softened her critique with a smile. "You can't stand not doing things your way."

"That's why I'm a consultant. I tell my clients what to do. Whether or not they implement my recommendations, they have to pay me." She grinned, then turned serious. "I'd get more business if I lost some weight."

Kendra nodded. "I know. It stinks."

"So help me out. Please."

Kendra chewed a bit of salad, swallowed and sipped at her water while she studied Norris. At last, she said, "I'm not kidding you. It's *hard*, physically and emotionally."

Norris wavered. She had compelling reasons for wanting to get skinny, but her professional drive always seemed to drain the energy from her personal life. This time, she had to stick with it. She took a deep breath. "I promise. I'll do whatever it takes."

"That's what you said last time."

Norris shrugged. That chic New England spa offered exercises, classes in nutrition, weight training, outside activities, Tai Chi, hikes and lovely massages. She'd timed her visit to be a leaf-peeper, taken long walks in vibrantly colored woods and lost several pounds. She'd gone home exhilarated and in a few weeks, gained the weight back.

"This time, I'll do it." She swallowed hard. "I have to. So how do I get into…what's it called?"

Kendra flicked a considering glance over Norris. "I'll ask, but it may take a while. They take people only on referral, and only a few at a time."

"Are they very expensive?"

"Absolutely. But look at it this way. With what you save on junk food, the program more than pays for itself."

"Chocolate? Recent studies say it's good for you."

"Forget it." Kendra laughed at Norris' horrified look. "After learning some new habits, you won't want it."

She doubted that, but hey, she had no choice. She had to get down to a smaller size. "How do they work? Drugs? Weird food like wood shavings and dandelion leaves?"

"Nothing like that, promise. They have a great chef." Kendra looked mysterious.

"So what is it?"

"Behavior modification same as any other diet program. You'll have to give up bad habits and learn better ones." She looked down at herself then gave Norris a satisfied smile. Yes, beautiful, thin and definitely mysterious. "It has its rewards."

"That's it? " Norris tucked a stray lock of hair into the clasp at her nape controlling her long hair. Lately it had been lusterless and wouldn't keep a style. It needed help, too. "How soon can we make this happen?"

"The program's not for everybody," Kendra said again. "It's tough. Maybe you'd better think about it."

"What's to think about?" Why was Kendra so reluctant? What was she hiding? Norris had to grin despite herself. Under that slinky wrap dress, there wasn't much Kendra could hide. What she'd give to wear something like that rather than her figure-forgiving suits. "Please. I've got to lose…well, I won't say how many pounds. I'm desperate, Kenny!"

* * * * *

Several weeks later, Norris entered the reception room on the top floor of an elegant high-rise. If she hadn't had an invitation card, written in exquisite calligraphy, she'd never have gotten past the lobby.

She looked around her with a great deal of curiosity. There were no windows, but none were needed. The lighting was soft, recessed, giving the lush ivory and taupe furnishings an inviting yet calming look. She released an uneasy breath and moved over plush carpeting to the Queen Anne desk where an underweight receptionist regarded her pleasantly. "I'm Norris Brownell. I'm here to register."

"Of course. We've been expecting you." The receptionist stood up. "If you'll have a seat, I'll tell the director you're here." Gliding away, she disappeared behind a door. Norris sank into an overstuffed chair, immediately regretting it. The seat was too narrow for her hips. She pried herself loose.

She'd had dinner with Paul and Kendra last night, and when she and Kendra had excused themselves to go to the ladies' room, Norris had tried to pump Kendra for more details.

Kendra was surprised she'd been accepted so quickly. "I had to wait six months for my reservation," she complained.

"I got a call last week," Norris said. "They had an unexpected cancellation and could fit me in." She shook her head. "I've been running like crazy to get everything organized."

"Why not wait?"

"No. I want to get this over with."

Kendra frowned. "Are you sure you're not being too impulsive?"

"Strike while the iron is hot, and all that jazz." Norris turned away from the mirror. "C'mon, Kenny, I'm starting tomorrow. Tell me what to expect."

"I wish I could." Kendra eyed her thoughtfully. "There's still time to back out."

"Why would I want to do that? "

"I'm worried about you. You may be starting, but how soon will you quit?"

That hurt. So she had an iffy track record when it came to sticking to a diet. She could do it if she wanted to. And this one, she really wanted to do.

Kendra took a second look at her expression. "Okay, sorry. I should be encouraging you." She propped a trim hip on the counter. "It's going to be hard. No kidding about that. Really hard, but if I got through it, you can do it, too."

Norris nodded, still uneasy with Kendra's half-hearted support. If she'd found it hard, could she herself stick with it?

Kendra liked getting up at the crack of dawn and running. She relished every moment under her comfortable down duvet.

Kendra didn't mind eating rabbit food. She lived by the motto, *Life is uncertain, eat dessert first.*

Kendra enjoyed hours at her gym. She'd rather have a massage.

But all that was going to change. She'd made up her mind. "If you can do it, so can I."

Kendra slid off the counter. "That's the spirit. I'll buy lunch in six weeks and we can compare notes. How's that?"

Norris blew out a breath. "You're on."

They'd hugged. Norris had gone home, feeling good about herself and now she felt her pulse pick up when the inner door opened.

"The director will see you now." The receptionist spoke courteously, but Norris detected the sneer skinny people reserved for anyone two ounces over perfect weight.

She followed her down a hall decorated in soothing earth colors, with framed artistic black and white photographs of thin women arranged at eyelevel along the walls. Norris slowed to look more carefully. None of the faces were visible, just backs of heads, profiles and all those perfect, slender nude bodies.

"Our clients," the receptionist explained.

Norris nodded. Her photo would be there, too. Thin and sexy, strutting her stuff.

She entered the door the receptionist held open for her and took the indicated seat before a long, pale wood table. The door closed behind her.

Alone, Norris felt free to look about the room. After the luxurious reception area, this one was a study in expensive minimalism. Apart from the table and the executive desk chair behind it, the side chair she occupied, and a flourishing fern in one corner, the room was bare. She squirmed on the uncomfortable seat.

"Ms. Brownell." A tall, thin woman in a severely cut black suit entered the room. "Welcome to *Sweet Discipline*." She extended her hand. Norris took it and cut the handshake short. Cold fish repulsed her.

The director opened a drawer on her side of the table and pulled out a folder. Opening it, she scanned the top page, then leafed through the remaining sheets. She raised cold eyes to Norris. "You were recommended by one of our clients?"

Norris gave her Kendra's name.

"Just so." The director studied Norris. "Did she tell you about our program?"

"Just enough to make me want to try it for myself."

"If you sign a contract with us, there is no backing out. No 'trying'," the woman warned in a dry voice. "We guarantee results, Ms. Brownell, but once you enter the program, you must stay to the end."

Norris hesitated. "I like to know what I'm signing before I commit myself."

"You saw the results with your friend? You read our brochure? You saw the photographs of satisfied clients on the walls?"

"Yes, but—"

The Director closed the folder and replaced it in the drawer with a soft thud. "If you are not committed to disciplining your body, there is no point continuing. We have very few openings and a waiting list. Someone else will be glad to take over your reservation."

Norris knew she was being manipulated. Every instinct told her to leave, but the remembered image of Kendra's slender body, and the happy, satisfied look on her face made her yearn for the same.

She squared her shoulders. "May I borrow a pen?"

The Director's mouth twitched in what might have been a triumphant smile. She retrieved the folder, opened it, and passed a multi-page contract to Norris. "Make sure you understand and agree to all the conditions before you sign." She handed her a black Waterford pen.

Norris settled back to read. The contract began in standard manner, specifying the participants, detailing the fee structure, and the stated goals of *Sweet Discipline*. Nothing out of line though the fees made her wince.

She read on. "Excuse me. What does this mean, 'accept all instructions and discipline without complaint or question'?"

"Just what it says. You are here to learn control of your habits. That requires a change in your behavior as well as your thinking. You must learn to discipline yourself."

Norris squirmed on the uncomfortable chair. The word *discipline* repeated so often troubled her. Maybe she should have paid more attention to the name of this exclusive spa. The clauses in the contract went on to stipulate that she would allow free access to her body. "Does this mean for massages?"

"Massages are part of the program. Exercise with a personal trainer is another."

That made sense. She'd often thought about hiring a private trainer but never seemed to get around to it. The clauses about confidentiality and nondisclosure made business sense. If the program could transform women's bodies so successfully, of course they wouldn't want competitors stealing their methods. "The refresher retreats are optional?"

"Many of our clients enjoy returning several times a year for maintenance. They want to make sure they are still on track."

Norris nodded. "Good idea." She scanned the next page and paused. She glanced up. "I won't have any socializing with other clients?"

"We find our clients do best when they focus entirely on learning new habits." She folded her hands on the desk and looked critically at Norris. "Most of our clients need no distractions. When you finish the day's activities, you will want to be alone to rest and meditate."

"Hmm. I'm not much for navel gazing."

The Director's lips twitched. "Neither are we. However, we do encourage thinking about behavior and how important it is to modify it. We emphasize a positive attitude."

"But...completely alone for six weeks?"

"Not alone. You will be with your trainer every day."

Norris furrowed her brow. "And if we don't get along?"

"We have provisions for that." The Director paused, then continued when Norris nodded. "Please note that while you are here there will be no distractions. You will have no visitors, receive or initiate no telephone calls, messages, email or mail. You will have no access or reason to use the Internet." The Director studied Norris' charcoal gray suit with a dismissive frown. "Have you cleared your schedule for the time required?"

Norris wished she'd worn her new Donna Karan suit. She lifted her chin. "My staff and associates have their instructions."

"Very good." The Director folded her hands on the desk. "Do you have any other questions?"

"Why wasn't I supposed to bring any clothes with me?"

"We supply everything our clients need."

"What if I absolutely must leave?"

"We strongly discourage that." The Director looked put out. "If you must leave early, you forfeit all fees but must still adhere to the confidentiality clauses."

Norris leafed through the contract again. Certain provisos still made her uneasy, but she needed this program. "When do I start?"

"When we are finished here, a technician will come for you. You begin at that moment."

"Okay, then." Norris initialed each of the contract pages and signed her name where indicated. The Director signed hers then dated the contract. She opened her drawer again and took out a receipt book. "Do you wish to pay by check or credit card?"

Norris handed over her platinum card. *This had better be worth it.* Mouth dry, she waited while the Director left the room to run the charge. A few moments later, she returned and handed Norris her card and the charge slip.

Norris gulped, signed and placed her card back in her purse.

The Director nodded. "Everything is arranged." She pressed a buzzer on the floor and in minutes, the door opened.

A slender but muscular woman in peach nursing scrubs smiled at Norris. "Ready? Come with me."

Norris swallowed hard. Ready or not, she was committed to *Sweet Discipline*. She stood, exchanged a look with the Director and followed the technician out the door. She glanced at the identification badge on her chest. "Angela. Hi."

The technician smiled. "I hope you enjoy your stay with us."

"Thanks. That's more than the Director said. Doesn't she have a name?"

"You won't see her again until you leave and she does an exit interview."

Norris rolled her eyes even as she recognized that Angela had not answered her question. It wasn't worth pursuing. If wondering about a name kept her awake nights, she could always find out. "That's a lot of mystery for a diet spa."

Angela giggled. "You'll see." She led Norris down several halls with doors marked Suite A, Suite B and so on. She stopped in front of Suite F and opened the door. "Here we are."

Norris halted in the doorway. This room wasn't sterile. On the contrary, it was as luxurious as any boutique hotel's penthouse suite. More so. Decorated in balmy tones of blues and greens, with a long cushiony couch just right for lazing, several large comfy-looking upholstered chairs, the living room had an immense, deep-piled area rug that made her think of oceans and far away places. She looked at the sign on the door and then at Angela. "Are we in the right place?"

"Oh yes. This is your private suite. Your bedroom is here," the technician advanced through the living room to gesture through an open door. "Your bath is connected." Retracing her steps, she slid open sliding doors to reveal a small but completely equipped kitchenette.

"Wow," Norris breathed. She reached into the small refrigerator for a chilled bottle of designer water. No wonder the fees were so high. She might have to work at losing weight, but she'd do it in comfort and style. "Where's the TV?"

"There aren't any in the suites. You might be able to use the one in the guest salon."

Norris shrugged. "What's in there?" she asked, pointing at a closed door on the far end of the suite.

"That leads to your private workout room." When Norris went to investigate, Angela stopped her. "Your personal trainer will explain all that after you've been introduced."

"Fine. When will I meet her?"

Angela gave her a sly grin. "You'll find some workout clothes in your closet. After you bathe and put them on, I'll take you to your trainer."

"I showered before I came."

"Your coach insists on absolute cleanliness. If you don't bathe now, you'll be sent back to do it."

"Weird."

"I'll wait for you out here. After your shower, don't put on any deodorant or cream. Leave your hair loose."

"Weird," Norris repeated but she headed for the bathroom, stopping along the way to admire the bedroom. "But nice," she murmured as she ran her hand over the silky azure duvet draping the king-sized bed. On either side of the bed, thick rugs invited bare toes. She carefully avoided glancing at the long bank of mirrors facing the bed.

No windows. She skirted the single armchair facing the bed to open a tall armoire and saw hanging space and several drawers. She opened them and found a set of teal exercise sweats in one, a number of sea-colored lightweight tunics in another and nothing in the last drawer. Was she supposed to wash her underwear every night?

She undressed and placed her clothes and purse in the armoire but left her earrings, watch and rings on the bedside table next to the latest bestseller she'd brought with her. Wearing only her bra, panties and control-top pantyhose, she went into the bathroom.

Marble everywhere. She looked forward to using the huge glass shower stall with multiple showerheads at various heights. Double sinks in a curving countertop stretched under a well-lit mirror. As usual, she averted her eyes from the sight of her near naked body.

A toilet and bidet were tucked demurely behind a half wall. Taking pride of place was a deep, jetted bathtub. Norris sighed, anticipating a long soak with scented oils.

She glanced at the toiletries and was surprised to find only soap, shampoo and hand lotion.

"Do you have everything you need?" Angela's voice floated in from the bedroom.

Norris went to shut the connecting door and found none. She narrowed her eyes, then shrugged. They were all women here. "I don't see any toiletries. I could use some conditioner, moisturizer and a few other things."

"There are toothbrushes and toothpaste in the drawer by the sink. You'll be provided with more later on."

Norris started the shower. She felt cheated. What spa didn't offer its own brand of scented soaps, oils, creams and lotions? Not even a loofah! Muttering to herself, she washed and shampooed quickly, then stepped out of the shower and whisked a towel off the heated bar. It was soft and heavenly warm against her wet skin. That was more like it!

"I left something for you to wear on the hook."

"Okay." Norris reached for her bra. She hated to put it back on, but she'd only worn her undies for less than half a day. Her bra and panties weren't on the counter where she'd left them. "Where's my underwear?" she called.

"You won't need it. I'll have it laundered for you."

Shaking her head, Norris pulled a lightweight aqua tunic over her head. It was cut low at the neck, revealing the cleft of her cleavage, and barely reached her upper thighs. "Is there a larger size in these things?"

"That's your size," Angela answered, coming to the bathroom door.

Norris tugged at the hemline. "I'll have to be careful if I do any bending over."

Angela giggled. "Better hurry. Your trainer doesn't like to be kept waiting."

Norris frowned. For the price she was paying, her coach had better get used to her convenience. Still, she opened the drawer, noted a comb and brush, disposable razors, tweezers, shaving cream and tooth-brushing supplies. She brushed and rinsed quickly.

With Angela watching every move, she ran the natural bristle brush through her hair and wished she'd kept her usual hair appointment. She needed a good cut to give her fine hair any shape or body. She'd been rushed getting everything squared away for her visit to the spa. Now she'd really need a trim when she was through here. Maybe she'd go for a whole new look to go with the new her. Maybe some artful streaking or highlights? Grinning, she gave her hair a last brush and left it loose as instructed. She wished she could wear at least some mascara. Without makeup, her eyes looked almost colorless, too light a green in her pale face.

"Lead on."

Angela looked her over, nodded in approval and left the bathroom. She stopped by the bed and gestured at Norris' jewelry and book. "If you'll put those in your purse, we'll store them in the safe until you're ready to leave."

"But I'm reading that book."

"You'll get it back later."

With a frown, Norris did as instructed. "Do I need shoes?"

"You're fine. Come with me. You're ready to begin your program."

At last! Now she'd get to the good stuff.

Chapter Two

Norris sat as directed on the high stool in the middle of an empty room. As Angela had warned, the lights went off, leaving her in total darkness. She didn't like sitting here in absolute silence. She felt edgy, disoriented, and certain she'd made a huge mistake in coming to *Sweet Discipline*. Kendra had warned her. Why hadn't she listened?

She was supposed to be using the dark to clear her mind, concentrating on the desire to change her body, to create new habits and strengthen her will to achieve her goals. Instead she clutched the edge of the stool, afraid to move, afraid she'd lose her balance and fall. She knew the floor was only inches below her feet. Rationally, she knew that, but the darkness surrounding her eroded her sense of proportion, making her feel suspended over a huge void. She could feel her heart thumping, her breathing becoming the only sound in that cool darkness.

There! What was that noise? She strained to hear better, but there was only utter stillness. Maybe she'd only imagined a door opening and closing, the soft rustle of clothing, a barely there suggestion of air against her face.

Her breathing quickened. "Is someone there?"

Silence. She leaned forward, trying to peer through the darkness. Nothing. Time passed, how much she didn't know.

Slowly, so gradually that at first she thought she was imagining it, she could see the color of her tunic. Pale at first, then deepening to aqua. Light! She looked around, upward, and then spotted a tiny pinprick of light in the ceiling. As she watched, it grew bigger, brighter until her entire body was lit, as if she were on stage, spotlighted before an audience.

The rest of the room was in darkness.

"Remove your tunic."

"What?" Norris gasped and whirled, almost falling as she spun on the stool. She tried to locate the speaker but as far as she could tell, she was alone. "Who are you?"

"Remove it." Relief that she hadn't been imagining things, that she wasn't in isolation any longer, vanished. The voice this time was peremptory, a deep baritone that left no doubt its owner could see her even if she couldn't see him. She registered the tone of his voice apprehensively. It was rich, smooth and totally cold, not a voice to cajole or coax.

"No way!"

"You agreed to follow all instructions. Now, for the last time, take off that tunic."

She clutched the fabric closer to her chest. "No."

Out of the darkness, a tanned male hand reached out and yanked. Her tunic tore easily, coming apart at the seams. Stunned, Norris grabbed at the fabric, but too late. The hand withdrew, leaving only a scrap of material to slither down her back and fall to the floor.

Flinching at the cool air wafting across her spine, Norris crossed her knees and covered her ample breasts with her hands. "What is going on here? Who are you? Get out of here!"

"I am your personal trainer," he said in a calm, even tone. "You will do everything I tell you to do, and you will do it quickly and to your best ability."

"But you're a man!"

"So I am. And you're a client paying for my expertise. You will begin by following my instructions."

"I expected a woman coach!"

"Your expectations are no concern to me."

She couldn't believe her ears. How dare he talk to her like that? She'd report his rudeness and get another coach. "I want to see the director, right now. I want someone else."

"No on both counts."

She heard him move back. He sounded as if he were to her right, but in the deeper darkness, he could be anywhere. She swiveled, looking for him.

"Get off the stool."

"Not until you get the director in here."

"She's occupied."

"Then you get me another trainer." Norris spoke slowly, forcefully.

"All the other trainers are with clients."

"The director assured me there were provisions for changing coaches."

"Did she?" he murmured, as though the provisions in the contract didn't apply to him. "You're stuck with me."

"Then I'll leave and make a reservation for another time."

"Suit yourself." His voice sounded indifferent. "But you'll lose your fees and you won't be accepted again."

Norris hesitated. She'd cleared her schedule for these six weeks. Her clients had grumbled, but she'd soothed them and given them a small discount on her usual fees. Fees. She'd paid an exorbitant amount to this spa. She could make it up, she supposed, and find another spa and diet program to lose the weight, but she'd been set on this one. Kendra had warned her the first few days were hard and told her she wouldn't last. *Oh, yes, she would.* She gritted her teeth. Just moments ago, she'd been wishing she'd listened to Kendra but now she was pissed. If Kenny could do it, she could, too. Whatever it took. Even if it meant listening to this odious man. For now.

"Well?" the odious man asked.

She held on for a moment, clinging to her dignity, then slid off the stool. It was hard covering her breasts and her mound at the same time, but she tried.

"Drop your hands." The voice came from behind her.

"Can't you stand still?" she complained. "I can't see you."

"Drop them."

From her left. So he was circling her, then. She turned her back and dropped her hands.

"Turn in a circle. Slowly." From behind, again.

She clenched her hands into fists as she turned. She couldn't see him, but she could feel his gaze on her. No matter how she moved, she could sense his looking at her, at every private part of her. Heat rushed to her breasts, to her neck and face. Her stomach wobbled as she turned. Oh, she shouldn't have had that last farewell slice of pastry...

"Stop." Now he was in front of her. "Stand still."

She lifted her chin. "You, too."

She thought she heard a soft chuckle. "In a moment someone will come in and take your measurements. Then we'll talk."

The door closed. The lights came on as the door opened and Angela and another woman, also in peach scrubs, entered. The other woman carried a clipboard. Neither one seemed concerned about her nakedness.

"Listen," Norris said urgently. "I have to speak to whoever's in charge. I don't want a man, that man!"

The women exchanged looks. "But he's the...one of the best trainers."

"I don't care. I want a woman coach."

Another exchange of looks. "Let's get your measurements and then I'll talk to the director for you."

Norris hesitated. She'd need to do this much for any trainer. "Okay."

Angela led her to a corner and pulled back a curtain. There was a scale, a desk and a number of instruments. "Let's weigh you first."

Norris stepped on the scale and closed her eyes. The other woman closed the curtain behind them.

"You have a lot of work to do," Angela murmured. "But you've come to the right place."

The other woman took up a tape measure and took her chest, waist and hip measurements. Angela wrote them down as Norris winced and tried to ignore the numbers. Then the woman took calipers and measured parts of her that made her eyebrows rise.

"Is that necessary?" Norris asked through gritted teeth.

"You'll want to know how much you've changed when you're through with the program."

Norris closed her eyes and submitted to more measurements. At last, the woman said, "We're done."

Angela whisked back the curtain. "We're through here."

"Good," the man with the baritone voice said. "You can go."

Norris hid behind the curtain and peeked out.

Angela handed him the clipboard, then whispered something. He looked at her sharply, then nodded. The two women left the room.

He sat one-hipped on the stool. He wore black, from closely cropped black hair down long legs to booted feet. Both hair and boots shone in the overhead light casting shadows on his face. Norris hesitated. He was attractive in an austere, remote sort of way. If she met him at a social event, she might take a second look, but that would be all. Still, there was something about him, something intriguing. Probably all his female clients developed crushes on him. She could see why they would, based on his looks and body alone, but he wasn't her type. So it couldn't be his chiseled, starkly handsome face, broad shoulders and lean body that made her breath come faster.

After all, he was an exercise trainer and he obviously spent time practicing what he preached. Broad shoulders and a flat waist went with his job. She'd expect him to be physically fit. It wasn't his looks, impressive as they were. She didn't go for tall, dark and handsome guys who loved their mirrors more than anything else. No, something about him, his aura or the stillness about him, warned her. By his presence, he dominated the space around him.

The fine hairs on the back of her neck quivered for attention. She retreated deeper behind the curtain and peered out at him.

He glanced up from her file. "Come here." He pointed to a spot in front of him.

"I asked Angela to get your supervisor. I want another coach."

"So she said."

"I'll just wait here until someone else comes."

"Suit yourself," he said evenly but he didn't budge.

Norris waited. He continued to leaf through the pages of her file.

Norris fidgeted. She cleared her throat.

He ignored her.

At last the door swung open. The director, with Angela at her heels, entered the room. "What is the problem?"

Norris stuck her head out from behind the curtain. "I want another trainer. A female coach. Not that man."

The director and the coach exchanged glances. He shrugged. Norris began to feel better.

The director approached her. "Ms. Brownell. Adrian is our most experienced trainer. You can't go wrong with him."

"He's a man," Norris hissed.

"So he is. He's also the one with the longest list of successful, satisfied clients, most of them women." She eyed Norris' disheveled hair. "Aren't you making too much of this?"

"But he made me take off my clothes!"

"How else is he going to evaluate your problem areas?"

"Well—"

"You're lucky to have him."

Norris flicked a glance from the cold-eyed woman to Adrian, who seemed to be ignoring their discussion.

"Well—" Norris said again, torn between her modesty and getting the best trainer on hand. Since she was here and she'd paid those outrageous fees, didn't it make sense to use the best they had? That's what she'd counsel her clients. Shouldn't she take her own advice? She blew out a breath. "Okay."

"Fine." The director turned to leave. "I trust you two will get along."

Adrian glanced up then, spearing Norris with a look. She interpreted it to mean that she'd better toe the line.

The moment the door closed behind the director, she had confirmation.

"Come out of there."

"I'm don't like being undressed." She also didn't like losing any confrontation.

"Get used to it." He paused a beat. "I'm waiting."

Let him wait! She was the client here. She deserved to be treated with respect and consideration. She couldn't let him see that she was afraid of him. Wouldn't give him the upper hand. Instead of letting herself be bullied, she'd treat him like she would any employee at a health spa. Sexless, there to serve her, someone she'd deal with only in an impersonal manner, even as they touched and toned her body. She'd forget his good looks, his deep, sexy voice and think of him as a doctor or nurse, trained to see the body as an instrument, a tool, not as a sexual being.

That was the key. Polite, but impersonal, interested in her only as a client. She could do that. He'd already seen all there was to see, much more than she'd ever allowed a man to see without the forgiving, concealing glow of candles and mood lights. If her trainer could help her trim down, make her body seductive and sexy, make her proud of her body, he could look all he wanted.

She stepped out from behind the curtain.

He pointed to his feet. "Here."

Like a faithful dog? She straightened her shoulders and strode forward. "Now, see here—"

"Look at me."

She glanced up, a long way it seemed in her bare feet. She saw a narrow nose and thin lips above a strong chin. His face was expressionless, his eyes dark and deep in the shadows. He looked powerful, in command and totally heartless. He was in absolute control of himself. Still, contained, only his chest moving with each breath he took. Norris shivered.

"I am Adrian. While you are here, you will be mine to train. You are the client, but I am in charge. Is that understood?"

She clamped her mouth shut. So he was the best. So she was lucky to work with him. All right. She was paying for his expertise. She nodded.

"Understand this. We have a variety of methods to choose from, depending on the client's needs and personality. The trainer customizes the method that will get the client involved. All our methods work," he stressed, "but the client has to work, too."

"It's no different than buying into and owning a project."

"Good." His grin was unexpected, quick and gone before she had a chance to enjoy it. "Then you'll have no trouble adapting to the program I've chosen for you."

A sudden shiver down her back warned her. "What kind of program?"

"Based on the number of diets and exercise programs you've started and never finished, you lack motivation in your personal life. I've developed a program to address that."

Okay, so they'd deduced from the multi-page questionnaire she'd filled out that she had little or no willpower when it came to rewarding herself with something yummy and gooey after a long day at work. That's why she was here. "That's good."

He flicked a glance at her. It was gone so quickly, she couldn't swear to it, but she was sure she saw amusement, a tiny sense of connection. That was good, too. It would make working together more pleasant.

"You will accept my instructions, follow them explicitly and treat me with courtesy." His gaze moved slowly over her body. "In return," he continued with a cool, implacable voice, "I will teach you respect for your body, discipline over your impulses. You will learn to control your thoughts and actions. You will achieve your weight loss goals."

Norris nodded. "That's what the contract says."

He lifted one finger to point it at her. Norris found herself distracted by it. His hands were tanned, as she'd noted before, but now she saw they looked strong, with a broad palm, yet with long, tapered fingers. Nails cut short, very clean. He wore no rings. "You need to improve both your physical and verbal self-control. Training will be as vigorous as needed."

That got her attention. Okay. She'd expected a lot of exercise. She'd never liked it, although she'd bought memberships in various gyms. Truth was, she hated the whole workout scene and never attended. She didn't get off on the no pain, no gain school of thought, but she could tough it out, even with a wannabe drill sergeant like him.

"You will be rewarded when you succeed, disciplined when you fail."

There was that *word* again, leaving a bad taste in her mouth. Discipline was punishment, and she'd never responded to deprivation. She ran her tongue over her teeth. "Disciplined how?"

He looked her over. "How do you define discipline?"

Norris tried to remember the dictionary's definition. "Um, keeping at something until you've got it right. Practice. Self-denial. Punishment." She licked her lips again. Ugh.

"You're on the right track. *Sweet Discipline* removes bad habits and helps a client substitute good ones, especially those of order, regularity, and obedience."

He sounded like he'd quoted those words many times before. Was this pet training or a damned expensive spa? "Obedience?"

He nodded. "To the goals you set yourself. To your inner self. To the program. To me." He paused while she thought about that. He must have interpreted the look on her face as resistance, which it was, for he added, "If you require help in creating or maintaining self-control, you will get it through discipline."

She swallowed hard. She searched his face, looking for another hint that he wasn't some robotron hired to spout the company line. That he was actually a human being under those intimidating black clothes. He was handsome, a beautifully formed male, and she couldn't find an ounce of humanity in him.

Come to think of it, the only real interaction she'd felt was with Angela, who'd giggled and talked to her like a person, not a child to be chastised for getting into the cookies. Or as something subhuman.

"Discipline takes many forms," Adrian said, reinforcing her growing perception of him as a coldhearted machine. "Mental, physical, emotional. Any method I choose will fit the infraction and you will accept and learn from it. Do you understand me?"

She hesitated. If she said yes, she'd be giving him permission to do...what? If she refused, what?

"Maybe I'd do better with another trainer after all," she suggested. She gave him a polite, hopeful smile. "Maybe you could switch with someone else? Man or woman. Even if they aren't the best?"

"Trainers are assigned according to a client's profile." He glanced at the clipboard in his hand. "Based on your answers on our questionnaire and your actions since you arrived here, you are temperamental and willful. You need me."

"That's ridiculous!"

He eyed her from head to foot. She was immediately aware of every ounce of fat, every bulge, every droop of her body. His gaze settled on her face. "Any trainer could work you through the physical part of our program. The mental and emotional part is harder. With your history, you need a firm hand."

"I'm not a child!"

"True. You're an adult and it's going to be harder to retrain yourself." He paused. "Your answer?"

She answered his question with one of her own. "How do you know so much about me?"

He paused, making her wonder if he'd answer. At last, he said, "We do our homework."

For an answer it lacked something and left much more to the imagination. What did they do, spy on her? The thought left a bilious taste in her mouth.

"I'm still waiting."

"I'm still thinking." Stay or leave and try another spa, another trainer?

No matter that she's just counseled herself to stay and get her money's worth, she could still walk out. Admit defeat. The image of Kendra's sleek body and smug look flashed through her mind. If Kenny could do it, so could she. After all, this man, this machine, would only be a part of her program. She could put up with whatever he dished out while she focused on the rest of the activities here. "Okay. All right."

He nodded. "First, you will learn respect. When you are with me, unless I tell you otherwise, you will kneel to me."

Her eyes widened. "You're out of your freaking mind!" This was a health spa, not some kinky club. When his expression didn't change, she knew he was serious. "What's kneeling got to do with losing weight?"

He blew out a breath. "Norris, I am going to say this only once. Our methods at *Sweet Discipline* are effective. Any of our clients will vouch for that." He spoke patiently, as if correcting a fractious child. "Any instruction I give is to help you achieve your goals. You are here to lose weight. You want your life to be more fulfilling, more pleasurable, more successful. Right?" He paused, as if giving her a chance to disagree.

She seethed at his reasonable tone, but couldn't argue with what he said. She imagined the awe on people's faces when she returned to work, skinny, sexy and successful. She imagined the impressed looks on her client's faces when she made a presentation. She imagined surprise changing into desire in Jack Rodriguez's eyes.

"I have never failed a client. I won't fail you."

She didn't like him but she believed him. After all, a place like this wouldn't attract any business if the clients weren't happy with the results. It was the same in her business. If his interpersonal skills ranked a minus ten, she could force herself to put up with them. The methods might be unusual, but all she was interested in was the final product. All she wanted from him was results. She blew out a breath and nodded.

"Very well. No more questions?"

"Not at the moment."

"I'll tell you whatever you need to know as we go along. Now, on your knees." His voice was inflexible.

Slowly, joints creaking, she lowered herself to the floor. "Ouch."

"Sit back on your haunches." When she did that, he added, "Now, place your hands palm up on your thighs. No, don't curl your fingers. Leave them open."

She flicked a glance up at him.

"You will keep your head lowered, eyes on the floor unless I give you permission to look at me."

This was too much. "Now, just a minute here—"

"You will not speak until I tell you to," he said harshly. "And when I speak to you, I want an immediate response. Understood?"

She blinked but lowered her eyes.

"Better. You are wondering why all this is necessary." She nodded. "Changing your usual positions opens your mind to change. Leaving your hands open signifies acceptance of change." He waited while she absorbed the concept. "To learn a new habit, you must get rid of the old one. To become a new person, the old person must go. Or, better put, pieces of the old person must go."

She could agree with that. There was a lot of her she wanted gone. His methods might sound crazy, but he'd promised he wouldn't fail her.

"Now, I have some questions. You will answer fully and truthfully."

All right, she'd expected to go into detail about her eating habits. The questionnaire had been long, very explicit, but there was always more to explain. She'd expected a disparaging look when she confessed her addiction to bread and butter, but on her aching knees, she wouldn't have to see his face. Maybe it would be easier this way. "Okay."

"Your name is Norris Aileen Brownell. You are thirty-two years old, a self-employed consultant. You specialize in human resource issues. You are unmarried though you were engaged once. He left you when you preferred your career to him." He paused to consult another page. "Still, you must have felt something for him since you suffered from depression for months. In consequence, you gained weight. You lost it while you were starting your business, and then gained more. What does that tell you?"

"How do you know all that?" she demanded.

He didn't answer, though it was increasingly obvious someone had done a thorough job researching her. "You are," he referred to the measurements Angela had taken. "Five foot seven," he glanced at her groin, "a natural brunette, and currently you are thirty-two pounds above preferred weight. Hmm, a pound per year."

He flipped a page. "You're generous to your friends, ambitious, creative in your recommendations. You are hard-working yet considerate of your associates. You support several charities and give them both time and money." He nodded approvingly. "You are also stubborn, like your comforts and are in need of personal direction."

He studied her face. "You're a complex woman, Norris. Many-sided, and some of them contradictory. Your family and friends have warm feelings for you, yet you have a smart mouth and a temper that gets the better of you. Outside this building, you are regarded with professional and personal respect."

Warmth flooded through her. Her shoulders straightened.

"Inside these walls, however, you are nothing. Nothing until you empower the inner woman, the one who can control herself and her destiny."

Warmth fled. Now resentment and anger warred inside her. "But—"

"I have not given you permission to speak."

She bit her lip to hold back her exasperation. She heard him turn a page, then another. "You don't exercise. You indulge yourself with food and alcohol. Given the choice of walking or taking a cab, you ride. In fact, you're quoted as saying walk is a four letter word." He studied her, as if cataloging her physical imperfections. "There is no suggestion that you use drugs."

"I don't. Never have."

"A point in your favor. However, you are lazy, indolent and disrespectful of your body."

She was really beginning to hate that deep voice detailing her flaws. What would he do if the positions were reversed, if he were down on the floor with his knees breaking and she stood above him reciting his faults? Taking comfort from the image of him cringing as she blasted his autocratic manner, his lack of personality, his coldness, she couldn't hide a smile.

"Something amuses you?"

She was silent.

"You may answer me."

Still, she said nothing.

"Very well. Your first deliberate act of disobedience."

She glanced up at him, letting him see her grin.

"And second." He stood. "You may rise. Come."

He walked to the door without looking to see if she followed him. It was only when she was two steps down the hall that she remembered she was nude. Too late now, but she walked more quickly.

He opened the door to her suite and once they were both inside her suite, he locked it.

That made her nervous. "Leave that door open."

Ignoring her, he crossed to the closed interior door, took a key from his pocket and unlocked it. He went in, flipped on the lights, turned and waited for her.

Uneasily, glancing at her bedroom, which belatedly she realized had no door, she moved toward him with apprehensive steps and pausing in the doorway, scanned the room.

He waited, saying nothing. She saw a large armoire on one of the padded walls and exercise apparatus like those she'd find in any upscale gym. A cycle, weight bench, treadmill, several machines and bits of equipment she couldn't identify but made her stomach hurt. There was also a metal bar stretching above her head from one wall to the other, a comfortable looking chair and an exercise mat on the floor. If all the client rooms were fitted out with individual exercise rooms and top-of-the-line equipment, no wonder the fees were so steep. She knew she'd be spending a lot of time in here. Ugh.

He gestured her to the middle of the room, then locked this door, too. How come he got keys and she didn't? The meaning suggested to her did nothing to ease her mind. She waited, discomfiture coiling in her as without a word, he went to the armoire, opened a drawer and brought out a pair of black cuffs.

This was outrageous! He could only mean to use them on her. She'd never been into the kinky stuff, bondage or domination. As he started toward her, she darted for the door. He was on her in an instant, grabbing her hands and in a flash, subduing her frantic efforts to pull away, he had the soft leather cuffs locked around her wrists. She cried out as he secured both wrists together.

She tried to twist free. She kicked out, landing a glancing blow on his shin. He grimaced, but said nothing.

She elbowed him, but he sucked in his gut and her elbow bounced off tight muscles. She cursed.

Ignoring her words, he stretched out a hand and brought the hanging bar down. He unraveled a chain wrapped about the middle portion, secured it to the ring on the cuffs and raised the bar until she was on tiptoe.

She couldn't believe it!

He'd tethered her to the bar.

Chapter Three

Norris gaped at him, mouth open, panting in surprise. He fixed the bar so that no matter how she tugged, she couldn't lower it. Wide-eyed, she watched him return to the open drawer and return with something black.

"Take these things off," she demanded and yanked at her chain.

He flicked her a glance. He didn't say a word.

She edged away from him as he moved to stand behind her. She kicked back at him, but standing on tiptoe didn't give her any leverage. He held her by the neck with one hand as he drew a smooth black leather hood over her head. She twisted her head this way and that, but that didn't slow him down as he tucked her hair out of the way and tied the drawstrings at the back of her head until the mask was secure. It covered her head and eyes, leaving only her nose and mouth clear. "Wait until the Better Business Bureau hears about this! And the cops!"

He stepped back, not even breathing hard while she panted as though she'd run a mile. "I'm sure they'll be very interested." He didn't sound worried.

She heard him pull the chair closer. He sat. Some nerve. Sitting comfortably while she hung like a Thanksgiving turkey!

"You're setting a new record, Norris. Very few clients reach this point within hours of arrival."

She grunted and tried to ease her shoulders. What did he mean *very few clients*? Was this standard procedure? Was this what Kenny meant about the first few days being hard?

"When you're calm and ready, we will start over."

"I'll scream! What will other clients think?"

"Suit yourself." He spoke calmly. "Though it might interest you to know that all the treatment rooms are soundproofed."

"Soundproofed?" she echoed, her voice rising in disbelief. "How can you get away with this?"

She heard tapping and thought he must be tapping his fingers on the arm of the chair. Maybe he wasn't as cool as she'd thought, not if he was giving in to a nervous gesture. Maybe there was a human being under that austere exterior.

"Let's get something straight here." He paused, waiting until she stopped trying to free herself. "Everything we do here is with our client's permission and cooperation. You signed the contract, giving us that permission. The cooperation is up to you."

"I never expected or agreed to this!"

"But you do expect to lose the weight and leave here looking like you want to look."

She said nothing.

"So now it's up to you. If you want to leave, just say so. I'll unhook you. You can get dressed and walk out the door. No one will stop you."

The only thing stopping her was her pride. How could she face Kendra after boasting she could stick with this diet spa? She'd have to admit she'd left within hours of arrival. Couldn't even last a day! Worse still, how could she face her staff or her clients?

"What's it going to be?"

"I didn't come here to be abused!"

"You recall the clauses about submitting to discipline?"

"But not this! This is abuse."

"This is only one method of getting your attention." He paused. "There are others more painful."

"Screw you!" She wrenched at the chain, and cursed when she achieved nothing but hurting herself.

He pushed her thigh. She swung to the side, increasing the strain on her arms and shoulders. Yelping, she bit her lip and swore. He pushed harder. Her toes left the floor for an instant while she scrabbled for balance. Pain shot from her fingertips to her toes. "Okay, okay," she gasped.

"Does this mean you are staying?"

She hesitated.

"If you want to leave, now's the time. If you're going to stay, you put yourself in my hands."

He'd said that before. His hands. The image of them, tanned, strong, with long slender fingers flashed through her mind. She'd liked the look of them and now, without her willing it, she wondered if there was any tenderness in them. *Tenderness?* In him?

He pushed her again. "I dislike being kept waiting."

"I dislike being hurt!" she retorted as she scrabbled to keep her balance. "All right." She took a deep breath. "Look, can we work this out? I'll do what I have to do and you treat me with courtesy."

"Courtesy. We can do that. If and when you earn it."

She blew out an exasperated breath. "And who will decide that? You?"

"Exactly."

She swore under her breath, calling him *bastard* among other things.

"I have excellent hearing."

"And sight no doubt," she muttered. "Like a big, black buzzard."

He laughed. "Are you suggesting you're dead meat?"

So he had a sense of humor. That and nice hands wouldn't get him very far. Still, it was better than nothing. "Get me down from here."

"Only if you're leaving. Are you?"

"No. I'm here to stay."

"Good for you." His approval eased some of her discomfort, but he made no move to release her from her cuffs.

"You've made your point. Now get me out of this."

"Not yet. Now it's question and answer time. Remember, nothing but the truth." He paused, as if waiting for her to protest again. "Why are you here?"

"I'm wondering that myself!"

He placed the flat of his boot against her thigh. "Try again."

It didn't take a genius to realize that he held all the cards. Until he let her down, she was at his mercy. But when he let her down... She held very still, composing herself, planning ahead. "To lose weight."

"Anything else?"

"To keep it off."

"How are you going to accomplish that?"

"Diet and exercise," she recited by rote. She'd heard the same thing from every diet counselor she'd ever consulted.

"Have they worked for you in the past?"

It was if he could read her mind. "At the beginning, yes."

"Then what?"

"Do I have to spell it out?"

He gave her a little push. She gasped out, "Then I get bored and cheat!"

"Is that your plan here?"

"No. I mean, how do I know what will happen?"

He chuckled. "With your success rate, I can guess that's exactly what you expect to happen."

He laughed? He laughed at her!

"But—" She felt the change in the air around her as he stood and came closer. The mask left her sightless, but enhanced her hearing and her sense of smell. She detected a clean, forest scent that was oddly appealing, considering how much she was beginning to loathe the smug bully. The heat from his body warmed her naked flesh. Her muscles quivered in the age-old dilemma of woman versus male. Stay or flee? But she was tethered, unable to help herself.

"That is not going to happen at *Sweet Discipline*," he said softly. "You will learn new habits of treating yourself with respect, treating your body with care, and if you have to absorb pain to do that, I will accommodate you. You will learn by instruction and practice to control impulses, your desires and satisfying those whims. In short, you will learn self-control."

Norris gulped.

"You will be pleased with the results. I won't fail you," he repeated. "In fact, I can guarantee you that all aspects of your life will improve."

She wanted to impress potential clients, her clientele and her associates. Jack Rodriguez in particular. "That's why I'm paying the big bucks."

"Don't forget it." He was very close to her, his breath clean and sweet. With her vision gone, her other senses came to life, including all her female awareness of him as a man. If she didn't hate him so much, she might be tempted to turn her head and find out how he tasted. Did he ever get it on with his clients? Maybe that was one of the unpublicized benefits. And it had been a long time…

"Do you have an active sexual life?"

Her breath whooshed out. How could he read her mind? Active sex life? No. Dull, sluggish, nonexistent? Yes. And worse still, it was her fault. Along with her once slimmer body, she seemed to have lost what few skills she'd had to attract men, much less lure them into bed.

"N…no," she admitted. The only activity her sex life had seen lately, besides her immediate and uncomfortable awareness of Adrian, were her fantasies of throwing Jack to the boardroom floor, jumping his bones and taking him so deep inside her, he'd never get free. Never want to, either.

"Why not?"

How humiliating! He'd already seen her body bared to him, did she have to expose the depressing facts of her sex life? It was embarrassing to admit that her age she had so little experience. Her weight was a turn-off for men, she knew that, but she hadn't always been this heavy. Even before she gained this weight she'd been a washout in the seduction department. She turned her head away.

"Don't make me repeat myself, Norris."

He didn't touch her, but she felt the threat. She licked dry lips. "Too busy, I guess," she mumbled.

"I don't believe you, but we'll let that go." As soon as Norris began to feel relief, he added, "For the moment."

He walked around her. Even without her vision, she knew he was looking her over. Like a side of beef in the meat market, she grumbled to herself.

"Are you hetero?"

Why did men always assume that if a woman wasn't busy servicing some man, she was lesbian? Was she? No. Had she ever wondered what it would be like to make love to another woman? Of course. What woman hadn't?

He touched her mouth with the tip of one callused finger. "Well? Men, women or both?"

She parted her lips. "Men."

He ran his finger down the valley between her breasts. When he paused, she urged him silently to go on, then stopped herself. It boggled her mind that she'd be here, naked, restrained with a mask over her head, letting a stranger touch her so intimately. Let? She wasn't *letting* him do anything! He stroked slowly down her belly, down below her navel. Her breathing slowed, waiting to see what he would do next. She swallowed, her mouth suddenly dry. His finger traced the edge of her mound. Oh, lower...lower... How could she be responding to him when he'd strung her up and...*ohmigod*, that felt so good!

"Would you like a satisfying sexual life?"

She flinched and tried to ignore the heat behind his finger just barely touching her curls. "Wouldn't everyone?"

He set her swinging again. Frantically, she pressed her toes against the floor. "Okay, okay!"

"Would you like to improve your sexual life?" he repeated.

"Yes," she whimpered as he stopped her swinging and the pain eased.

"Are you willing to learn what it takes to make it happen?"

All it would take was to lose those pounds and get the hell away from here!

"Are you?"

"How?"

"Yes or no?"

"Yes, dammit!"

"Then I will teach you that, too."

"*You?*"

"I am your trainer in all things."

"No way! I'm not attracted to you." Okay, so she wasn't quite truthful with that one, not after the way she'd responded to the way he touched her, but sex? No way! "For sure I don't like you."

"That's not important. Along with adopting some exercise habits, you'll learn intimate techniques. When you earn your rewards, it won't matter who taught you."

She shivered. "What rewards?"

"I ask the questions."

Norris hesitated. She eased her weight from one foot to the other, stretching both her body and her viewpoint. If Adrian could teach her to seduce Jack, it would be worth whatever she had to go through. And no one would ever know. Client confidentiality worked both ways. She ran her tongue over her dry lips. Nodded.

"I have some instructions for you. Listen carefully." His voice was crisp, impersonal, as if she hadn't just agreed to have sex with him. Sex with the man who'd bound her? Hurt her? Talk about kinky!

"First, you will wear a tunic when you are outside your rooms. Otherwise, you will be naked. "

"Why? So you can get your jollies?"

"My 'jollies' are my own concern. Being naked will help you remember your body at all times."

"As if I'll forget how much I hurt!"

"Your pain level will be your choice." He paused to let her consider that. When she said nothing, he continued, "You will be clean at all times. This may mean several baths or showers a day as I decide."

Okay, she'd expected massages and mud baths. She could live with that. She nodded.

"Your body will be mine to treat as necessary."

Uh-oh. This one, no matter that she'd signed that damn contract and had just agreed to sex, this one made her uneasy. Being tethered was more than enough. What else did he have in mind? She started to ask, but he overrode her voice.

"Next, to learn respect for your body, you must be respectful. You will speak only when I give you permission. If you wish to say something, you may attract my attention by placing one finger beside your mouth.

Like this." He demonstrated, his long index finger resting beside her lips, facing inward. His finger was hard and warm. It was living proof that he was there with her, flesh and blood, not some heartless robot. She wished she could see him. Feel more than his finger. She parted her lips, as if inviting his finger in.

He stepped back. "As I indicated before, you will kneel in my presence. You will keep the position I taught you earlier, but you will sit with your back straight and your chin tucked in.

"You will look at me only when I give you permission.

"If you are in need of anything, you will ask me and if I agree, I may grant it."

This smacked more and more of submission and domination, something she'd read about, but hadn't ever experienced. She considered what that might mean. Her breasts tingled as she remembered some of the racier things she'd read. Bondage and physical restraints. Well, wasn't she experiencing that right now? It hurt when she moved, and she felt powerless, tethered as she was to the bar above her head. He'd trussed her up here with no problem, proving he was stronger than she. If she had to ask for permission for what she wanted, that meant giving him additional power over her. Could she do that? Give up control over her body to a man she'd labeled odious and a bully not long ago? But then, there had to be something in submitting to someone else that kept people coming back for more. She'd heard that there was a tremendous sexual satisfaction in submission and domination. If she agreed to Adrian's demands, would she find some of that satisfaction for herself?

"From now on, I will be the only person you see. I will be everything to you."

She frowned. She'd taken it for granted that she'd be working with other people. Masseurs, skin care specialists, manicurists, and a dietician. Those were staff she'd find at any spa. But just him? That might be too intense. Her heart raced.

"Your meals will be brought to your room. You will not speak to the person who delivers them. When I give you permission, you may eat and drink what I allow." Her protest died in her throat when he nudged her into another swing. Her wrists ached.

"If you disobey any of these instructions, or others I give you during training, you will be punished until you learn to discipline yourself."

Fear rippled down her spine.

"You take my meaning. Good. I don't enjoy giving pain, but I have no scruples about administering it. What you're experiencing now is only the smallest example of what you might expect."

She believed him. He'd been successful in demonstrating who had the upper hand, coolly trussing her and letting her hang while he sat comfortably.

"On the other hand, as you go through training and succeed at your tasks, you'll be rewarded. One hand," He ran his finger along the tendons of her left hand. "Discipline and pain. On the other hand," he murmured as he traced the curve of her right arm from wrist to armpit. Her skin quivered as she waited for him to touch her breast. "Success means rewards. Good feelings about yourself and your efforts." She swallowed, eager to feel a taste of that particular reward.

He stepped away. "The choice is yours."

She bit back a groan.

She felt him check the handcuffs then heard him move to the door. "I'll be back later."

"You're going to leave me like this?" she wailed.

"Think about the choices you want to make.

He was through the door while she still spluttered. How could he leave her alone? And more important, when was he coming back?

She tried to roll her shoulders. That didn't work. She tried standing on one foot, then the other, but that didn't relax the cramping in her legs. She tried to blank out her discomfort with thoughts of what she'd be doing if she hadn't listened to Kendra and come to *Sweet Discipline*.

Damn Kenny!

For a few moments, it felt good to blame her friend for her predicament, but it was nobody's fault but her own. Kendra had warned her. She'd disregarded that warning and insisted Kendra recommend her. Even at the last moment, Kendra had cautioned her. So now, she had no one to blame but herself.

She was here because she wanted to be here. She'd made a deliberate commitment to changing her body, her outlook, and her future. She wanted to change. She kept telling herself that. She'd envied Kendra her svelte and sexy figure and wanted the same for herself. And that went double for Kendra's very active sex life. What wild sex had Kenny been talking about? New positions? Had she also learned new techniques while she was here?

What was Adrian going to teach her? She couldn't ignore being aroused when he talked of sex. Sex with him? How?

Was it possible to have sex while she hung like a slab of meat?

If Adrian put her legs around his waist, supported her while he thrust into her... She imagined how it would feel, unable to do anything but take his banging into her, do nothing but clamp him within her thighs and pull him closer.

Heat, then moisture gathered between her legs. Her hips moved with imagined thrusts. Was Adrian hard? Long, thick? What was he like as a lover? Would he satisfy her or be interested only in his own pleasure? Maybe he got off on arousing clients and then leaving them to stew, frustrated. Just like this. The thought made her angry.

She wouldn't think about him as a man with his own sexual needs. She'd use him like any piece of equipment in this room. She'd absorb what he could teach her and then use it for her own needs.

She closed her eyes and mentally superimposed Jack's face over Adrian's. Yeah, that could work. Many women fantasized making love with another man while having sex. She could do that. She'd think about Jack and what she wanted to do with him.

Time passed. She thought about sex, deliberately focusing on her fantasies and visualized making them real with Jack Rodriguez. Not Adrian. Jack. Jack's buff physique and trim belly under his custom suiting had attracted her since they'd met. She'd fantasized about having his manicured hands on her breasts, wondered how his gym-toned body would taste. She ran her tongue over her lips, imagining hot words and even hotter actions. Heat liquefied between her legs.

When she got out of here, she'd make his tongue drop. Make him drool over her. Make him fantasize about making love to her the way she'd dreamed about him. And when it happened, look out. She'd use all the stuff she learned from Adrian to blow his mind. Oh yeah!

Her stomach grumbled. She'd lost all track of time. Was it time to eat? Her stomach cramped. How could she think of food when she was aching all over? So this was how they intended to modify her behavior. Make her hurt so much she couldn't think of anything but her pain. By the time that dictator Adrian came back, she'd have melted off five pounds at least.

Norris rested her head against her outstretched arm. She counted to one hundred, then one thousand. She listed her favorite foods, rearranging the top ten as the list grew. Carrots and celery were way at the end. Cream Puffs, French Onion Soup, pizza, a thick steak, mmm, now that was food.

She thought of her soft, comfortable bed, the book she'd been reading, and her favorite TV shows. Wouldn't it be nice to be propped up in bed now with some tea and cinnamon toast? Followed by some chocolate truffles... That just made things worse.

She thought about Jack and what he might be doing. Maybe he was at his gym, buffing those muscles until they bulged. Wouldn't he be surprised if he could see her now? Would he rush to rescue her, or leave her hanging like a bloated whale? That thought made her insides hurt and she quickly replaced it with the admiring glances she'd get when she returned to work.

Soon, though, nothing blocked the pain. She fought it, cursed it, cursed Adrian, screamed, and then gave in to it and endured. Slowly, so gradually, and in barely discernable increments, the pain ebbed. She felt it recede as if she were floating, now on the surface of a gentle sea, now on puffy clouds looking down on an expanse of deep, dark blue.

Time passed, she didn't know how much. At times she thought she smelled food, other times she thought she heard voices, but when she lifted her head, she was still in the dark, still alone, still suspended from the bar. Music drifted by, low relaxing tones, and she absorbed it into her mind.

Time passed.

Chapter Four

She didn't realize Adrian had returned until he lowered her arms. She groaned as blood and pain rushed through them. He removed the mask and silently helped her through the door to her living room, then into the bathroom. The bright light hurt her eyes.

She felt heat, then tendrils of steam around her body. She opened her eyes as he led her to the tub and helped her into the steaming water.

Her bunched muscles screamed as she sat, then slowly unfurled and eased with the heat. He turned on the jets and as the water rushed around her aching body, she let him push her back until only her face was above the water.

She couldn't speak, only feel. He took a washcloth and wet and soaped it. Without a word, he began to wash her, competently, unhurriedly. He lifted one arm and washed it in long strokes, massaging sore muscles as he cleansed her. He did the same for the other arm, then her legs. She moaned in relief as her cramped muscles responded and relaxed.

It felt so good, even as he soaped and rinsed higher and higher on her thighs then she began to notice how else her body was reacting to his sure touch. She murmured a protest when he lifted one leg and washed between them.

"Quiet."

She bit her lip and tried to ignore the warmth of his hand, detectable even against the heat of the water. She felt the washcloth against her labia, felt his finger wrapped in terrycloth penetrate her, circle her pussy, then retreat to thrust in again. She bit her lip against the unexpected pleasure, then relaxed and accepted. He washed her intimate folds, pulled gently at her clit, and then raised her buttocks to wash her bottom. She tightened against his finger penetrating her ass, then winced as he flicked a finger hard against her clit in unspoken reprimand.

When he re-soaped the washcloth and ran it again back to her ass, she remained still, trying not to tense as his cloth-wrapped finger wormed its way into her. He massaged the inside of her anus, surprising her with the way it made her feel. Excited. Eager.

She risked a glance at him. His face was devoid of expression. He could have been somewhere else entirely for all the interest he showed.

From nowhere came a flash of resentment. He was male! The least he could do was pretend some interest in her as a woman. He could pretend he enjoyed arousing her How could he ram his finger up her ass as if it meant nothing?

He let her leg plop into the water with a small splash. He dropped the washcloth, and lathered his hands. With care, bare-handed, he washed her breasts, shoulders and underarms, adding a muscle-deep massage as he kneaded away her lingering pain. Along with the pain, her indignation eased, replaced with a fresh awareness of her body. She could almost imagine he was her lover, stroking her in foreplay, arousing her to almost unbearable excitement. Not that she'd ever had a lover do that, but she could dream.

She forced an eyelid open. He was attractive in a chiseled, masculine way. Seen this close, his eyes, which she'd imagined to be as black as his hair, were brown. A warm, chocolate brown. Too bad they belonged to this severe, humorless tyrant. Even his hair, clipped short, added to his austere look.

But oh, he did have good hands. His fingers worked on the sore muscles in her upper arms, drawing from her both pain and resistance. Remembering to put a finger beside her lip as he'd instructed, she sighed. "That feels good."

She barely heard his response. "Wait until tomorrow."

* * * * *

For sure that was one way to lose weight. Exhaust the clients into oblivion, then watch them waste away to nothing. She wished she had a scale to see just how much she'd lost, but there wasn't one anywhere in her suite. She'd asked the woman who delivered her breakfast if she'd bring her one, but the woman had shaken her head, said nothing, put down the tray and left.

Norris spooned another grapefruit segment into her mouth. She hated grapefruit but this morning, it was heaven. Sleep had restored her appetite and her resentment about the way she'd been treated so far at *Sweet Discipline*. All her rancor was directed at one person, the man who had subjected her to humiliation and pain. After her experiences yesterday, she determined there were going to be some changes around here. After all, she was the client and deserved to be treated with respect and care.

The hall door opened.

"Be with you in a minute," she said without turning to look.

"Norris."

At the sound of displeasure in that deep baritone, she knew she was in trouble. She scooped up the last sliver of dry wheat toast and turned, still chewing.

"Norris."

She felt her heartbeat pick up speed. How could he do this to her? She hated feeling like a child with her hand in the cookie jar. What now?

He pointed a finger at the floor. What? Oh, that stupid kneeling routine. She hesitated, then thought that the sooner she indulged him, the sooner she'd get busy with her program. She slipped off the chair onto her knees. She fumbled with the edge of her tunic, trying to pull it down her thighs. Flabby thighs.

"Be still. Did I give you permission to eat?"

Angry with herself for feeling cowed, she glared at him. "I was hungry."

"No doubt. What did I tell you yesterday?"

She flicked a glance at him, but said nothing. Today he wore plain gray sweatpants, a black T-shirt and athletic shoes. The fabric clung to his shoulders and followed the outline of his flat abs. The material in his pants draped over his package. Her gaze settled on the shape of his penis under the loose fabric. Her mouth went dry.

"Your time at *Sweet Discipline* is going to be difficult until you lose some bad habits. It's your choice. Easy way or hard way."

"*Sweet Discipline*, my ass! They should have called it *Abandon Hope Spa*."

He chuckled. "I see your sense of humor hasn't deserted you. You're going to need it."

She needed more than that. She needed to feel good about what she was doing. She needed encouragement and support, but he made her feel small. Last night, she'd fallen asleep reminding herself of her goals, and bolstering her resolution to do whatever it took to lose her weight and gain control of her life. And here she was, on her knees, feeling humiliated and awkward.

"You are to be naked in my presence," he reminded her.

"You have your clothes on," she retorted.

"Stand up. Go brush your teeth and come back naked."

A few minutes later, she found him in the training room. He pointed to the floor at his feet. Reminding herself that she'd leave here skinny and sexy, she took her position at his feet.

He lifted a foot and placed it on her neck. She felt the treads on the sole of his shoe as he pressed her body down. She put out her hands to balance herself but he had her nose to the floor in an instant.

He kept her in that humiliating position while he spoke in a dry, unemotional voice. "It takes several days to make new habits. At the rate you're going, it may take you a week or more, but you'll make them."

"Okay, okay. You made your point."

"The question is, Norris, are you going to fight me every inch of the way, or submit?"

His foot grew heavier on her neck by the second. Her instincts yelled, *Fight, fight*! Her ego refused to let him get the better of her. This wasn't learning new habits. This was cruelty. Sadist! She squirmed. She hadn't signed up for this. She wanted to be thin and in control of her eating, but this was too much!

He waited. Her breasts, squashed to the floor, hurt. Her ass, pointing up to the ceiling, quivered. Her practical side reminded her of the charge on her credit card.

She gulped. "Okay, you win."

His foot didn't move. "You submit to me? Say it."

She couldn't move her head, couldn't move. She was forced to say the words. "Yes." She swallowed. "I submit to you."

The pressure on her neck eased immediately as he lifted his foot, but came back on her ass as he moved his foot there and crushed it to the floor.

"Don't move." He cautioned her. "Not until I tell you."

She nodded.

"What is the rule about eating?"

"Wait until you tell me to," she answered, her voice small but rebellious.

"And about the food you eat?"

"Only what you tell me to eat."

"What is the rule about speaking?"

"Only when you give me permission."

"Very good. Will you remember all that?"

"Yes."

He removed his foot. "You may kneel."

She scrambled to her knees, lowered her head, straightened her back and placed her hands, palms up, on her thighs.

"Very good." His voice was still emotionless. "Stand and go to the mat."

She waited by the mat for further instructions.

"We will begin with some basic exercises. Stretches first."

He led her through the routine, correcting her stance, pushing her until her muscles relaxed and lengthened. She panted and muttered under her breath.

"Stop."

Gratefully, she crumpled onto the mat, breathing hard.

"You are out of shape." He said it without expression, but she winced.

"Get up. Drink some water." He pointed at a small refrigerator on a shelf. She dragged herself up and over to the fridge, grabbed a bottle of spring water and drank heartily.

"The only reason you may stop a training exercise is for water. You will not allow your body to become dehydrated."

She gurgled down the last drop, then nodded.

"Return."

She dropped to her knees again in front of him, expecting praise. Instead, he ordered her to stand and put her through another series of exercises.

"I hate this," she gasped through clenched teeth.

"Another set for speaking without permission."

It seemed like hours later when he called a halt and ordered her to drink again. She paused at the fridge. She started to ask if he wanted one, then remembering that extra set of exercises, merely lifted one to him in invitation.

"No. Drink that, then shower. Come back in five minutes."

"Five? I can't do—"

"Four minutes."

She ran for the bathroom. The hot water streaming over her head and body from the strategically placed showerheads felt good, so good, she was tempted to relax and take a leisurely shower. A massage. Scented oils, candles, quiet music. Ah…

She hopped out of the oversized shower, dried quickly, brushed her teeth again and returned to Adrian.

"You're forty-five seconds late."

Norris dropped to her knees in front of him. He made a small noise in the back of his throat that she hoped was approval.

"On the treadmill."

When she was there, he commanded, "Walk, then run. Start slow."

Oh, no. She hated to run, hated to feel her boobs bouncing up and down. She hesitated, giving him a pleading look.

"Run."

She shifted her weight from foot to foot. "I won't say it again."

She moistened her lips, threw him a resentful glare and turned the machine on. One foot, the other, bounce, bounce, jiggle, jiggle.

"This is not good for the breasts," she muttered. "I should be wearing a sports bra for this."

He flicked a glance over her breasts. "You'll survive. Pick up the pace for talking."

She held on to the balance bars and picked up her pace, glaring at him for his callous remark. "It hurts."

"Think of it as incentive. When you lose the weight, your breasts will firm up. You might not need a bra then."

She grumbled, but fitfully, since breathing and talking at the same time was hard.

He watched her, checking her respiration and her endurance. He turned the machine up a notch. "Faster."

Monster, sadist, lecher! All these and more she called him silently, even as she panted and ran.

He watched, a smile she couldn't classify on his lips. For a moment she thought she saw approval, even assurance, but that couldn't be. Damn him! He enjoyed making her suffer. And she'd promised to let him touch her sexually. She must have been out of her mind!

"Pick up your knees. Higher."

She white-knuckled the bar, lifted her knees and ran, gasping now. Those pounds had better be dropping like flies because any moment now, she'd fall off the treadmill flat on her ass.

"Slow down." She did as he instructed, slowing until she barely walked. "Stop." He turned the machine off. "Drink."

Oh, she was tired of those terse commands, rapped out in that heartless voice. She staggered to the water, took a long drink, then wiped the sweat from her face with her forearm.

"That's it for now. Clean yourself and wait for me in your bedroom."

Her eyes widened. She glanced at him, wondering what to expect. Did he expect her to have sex with him? *Now?*

He held her glance, then deliberately looked up at the rod and chain hanging from the ceiling, then back at her.

She fled.

When she came out of the bathroom, still toweling her hair dry, she found him sitting in the armchair facing the bed. He had all his clothes on, thank goodness. He looked comfortable and at ease, legs spread with one ankle resting on the other knee. Behind him, the mirrors reflected the back of his dark head and the powerful set of his broad shoulders.

Again, she was aware of her nakedness. She didn't feel sexy, but insignificant and powerless. She hated that, hated him.

"Come here."

She lowered the towel, as if accidentally covering her body from his gaze, and took several steps closer to him. She saw herself in the mirror, flabby and jiggly, her skin pink from her hurried shower, her hair still dripping onto her shoulders, and quickly averted her eyes.

"Assume the position."

She dropped to her knees in front of him and waited for him to speak. When he did, her mouth dropped open, her chin lifted, she stared up at him. Her gaze dropped to his crotch. Beneath the sweatpants, his penis made an unmistakable bulge.

"Do I have to repeat myself?"

She swallowed. Shook her head. Still, she couldn't speak. Or look away.

He sighed. "All right, let's start with something easier. When did you lose your virginity?"

She moistened her lips. "I was seventeen. Later than most of the girls I knew."

"Tell me."

"All my friends were doing it. I felt left out."

"Only the physical details."

"He pulled my bathing suit off. First, the top. Then the bottom, and yanked me on top of him. He pinched my breasts and pushed in. He held me by the hips." She found it easier to talk if she spoke to his athletic shoe. "It hurt."

"Did you climax?"

She concentrated on the way he'd tied the laces. "I didn't even know what it meant."

"So you didn't. Your first sexual experience was painful. Humiliating?"

Oh, God, yes. She'd worried for a week until she'd gotten her period. She'd avoided the boy at school, tried not to hear the gossip recounting his bragging or see the speculative looks turn scornful when he rated her a zero.

"Now tell me about the last time you had sex?"

"It wasn't much good." She'd rated that guy pretty damn low.

"Forget the commentary."

"He came, I didn't. I was dry, and it hurt."

"Not much different than the first time." She risked a glance upward to see him watching her with an unreadable expression.

"Now the best sex you've had."

She paused, remembering the cruise and the steward who more than earned his tips from women traveling alone. When they didn't find romance in the public salons, they settled for hot and heavy sex with the steward. Just as she had done. It hadn't been very good at first, but the steward had persisted, making her come repeatedly. He'd earned a very, very large tip.

"I'm waiting."

"I came a lot," she said at last.

"That's it?"

She nodded.

"I see we have a lot of work to do."

If the result was looking like Kendra, sleek, sexy and sated, she'd do anything. "Okay."

He chuckled. "I wasn't asking your permission."

He had a pleasant sounding laugh, but she didn't like the feeling it gave her. Like his voice, his laughter was rich and smooth but this time, instead of coaxing her into laughing with him, it made her feel self-conscious. Somehow less worthy. So what if she hadn't slept around? She was entitled to be choosy. As she considered that, she had to admit that her inexperience wasn't due to her selectivity, but a lack of willing partners. Or lately, one in particular, Jack. But that could and would change. When she left *Sweet Discipline*, she'd knock him off his feet. And flat on his back. In her bed.

"Do you masturbate?" he asked, repeating the question that had shocked her.

This time, she didn't flinch. She wasn't going to give him the satisfaction of hurting her feelings. "Sometimes."

"How?"

What did he mean how? With her fingers and her trusty vibrator. What else was there?

"Show me."

Her head snapped up.

"Spread your legs and show me how you make yourself come."

"I can't! Not with you watching me."

"You can and you will."

"Please don't make me do this."

"Do I have to remind you that you gave me your submission?"

She flinched. Then, slowly, her fingers trembling against her thigh, she reached between her legs and touched herself. She was a bit moist yet from her bath, and her labia separated easily. Tentatively, she stroked, finding the sweet spot that always worked for her. In moments, she felt more moisture gathering.

"Stop."

She obeyed, but reluctantly. Why was he having her do this to herself if he was going to stop her just when it was getting good?

"Are you close?"

She nodded, suddenly dry-mouthed.

"Slow down. Make it last."

She tried to obey, but lasted only a few more strokes. She came quickly with a small shudder.

"Is that the best you can do?"

What was wrong with it? She did as he'd said and made herself come. She looked at him.

"You've showed me that arousal isn't a problem for you."

True, she could turn herself on. She just couldn't manage turning Jack on. Maybe that's what Adrian had in mind. He could teach her how to arouse a man.

"Now you need to work on control."

Whose control?

"Get up. Open that drawer." He pointed to the lowest of the armoire drawers. "Bring the bag here."

"What bag?" The armoire had contained only her spa outfits this morning. Who had put something in there since then?

She opened the drawer and sure enough, there was a travel bag, monogrammed with the spa's logo. She picked it up. It was bulkier and heavier than it looked and she took it to him as instructed, then knelt at his feet again.

"Open it."

She unzipped it, and reaching in, she pulled out a number of packages wrapped in the spa's distinctive cream paper. All right! Goodies.

"Some clients may get these supplies later in their training, but with you, I am making an exception." She glanced up, puzzled. "Open them."

She pulled the heavy wrapping paper away from an oblong package. A set of dildos, in varying sizes, was nestled inside a clear plastic case. *What?* She'd been expecting toiletries, the spa's signature lotions and creams. Why these dildos? Heat rushed to her cheeks as she studied them. The smallest was no bigger than her index finger, slender and straight. Another was longer, slightly curved. The third was longer, larger all around, with a bulbous tip. All three were wider at the base. She glanced up at him. "Why—"

"We will discuss their uses later. Open another one."

Anticipation and a curious sense of dread trickled through her, making her skin feel hot and too tight. It felt so strange, sitting here at Adrian's feet with these sex toys in her hand and her body so aware of his. She flicked a glance up at his face and saw his eyes intent on hers, an unreadable expression on his face. Yet, there was something deep in his eyes. Warmth? That was crazy. It was only her own flush that made her see heat in his gaze. Discuss, he'd said, but she was positive he meant to do more than talk. Her breath hitched in her throat. She hesitated, her hand poised over the open bag.

He prodded her with the tip of his shoe. Quickly, she reached in and brought out another package. Unwrapping it, she found a vibrator; similar to the one she had at home, made of soft, flexible rubber and shaped like a penis, complete with veining and a ridged head. She couldn't stop the involuntary look at his crotch, wondering how the vibrator compared to the real thing.

He noted her look but said only, "Open the rest."

Obeying him, she found a small black velvet box containing a set of silver balls connected by a red ribbon. She knew what they were but had never used them. Her breasts felt hot. Her internal muscles clenched as though the balls were already deep within her. She looked at him again, noted how his eyes shuttered his expression, but he couldn't hide the way his tongue flicked over his lips, or the way his Adam's apple moved in his throat. It excited her to know that he wasn't immune to her increasing stimulation. She hadn't thought of him as a sexual partner when she first met him. Quite the opposite. His looks had intrigued her, but his severe, uncompromising attitude had nipped any attraction in the bud. Yet here she was, very much aware of him as a man. An increasingly sexy, attractive man.

She put the Ben Wa balls aside and picked up the last package. Slowly, prolonging the moment, keeping an eye on his reactions, she peeled back the wrapping paper. Inside, a double pronged vibrator lay nestled in plastic wrap. One of the prongs was shaped like a very large penis, the other, smaller one was thinner and slightly curved. Was it really supposed to go into her pussy and her ass at the same time?

She raised a questioning look. He nodded, this time his heated gaze fixed on hers. There was no doubt in her mind. He really meant to use all those dildos on her! She had trouble swallowing as she lowered her head, hiding her excitement and fear from him.

"These are for your pleasure. They are also teaching instruments." He waited a moment, as if gauging her reaction. "I will allow you to choose one now. After that, I decide."

Her hand hovered over the assortment, then holding on to the familiar, touched the penis-shaped vibrator.

He reached into a pocket, lifting his hips as he did in a gesture that seemed as though he was offering himself to her. Her eyes locked on the unmistakable bulge at his crotch. So he wasn't immune to the sex toys! Was he going to use them to play with her? He pulled out a handful of batteries, selected two and gave them to her.

"Show me how you use that."

In her nervousness, she inserted the batteries wrong, had to pull them out and try again. She turned the switch and the vibrator buzzed and oscillated in her hand. Taking a deep breath, she applied it to her clitoris. She shuddered and exhaled slowly. It felt so good! She'd come only minutes ago, but this was even better than her fingers.

"Stop."

She couldn't hold back a frustrated moan.

"Stretch out on the rug."

She did, with her body angled away from him.

"So I can see." He spoke not as a potential lover, but with clinical detachment.

Blushing, she changed position, lying in front of him, knees open and bent, exposing herself to him. When he nodded, she touched herself again with the vibrator. Here, stroking herself along one side, then the other, from the bottom of her opening up to the little bud, hesitantly, ashamed to be turning herself on again in front of him.

In a moment, that didn't matter. She closed her eyes and forgot Adrian watching her. She forgot her humiliation of exposing her most private parts. She forgot all but the pleasure building and building inside her. She was so close! She turned the vibrator, inserting the tip into her eager pussy, panting with excitement at the thought of something, even her vibrator, filling her, satisfying the ache within. She moaned and half-opened her eyes.

Suddenly, his hand swooped down and took the vibrator away. Startled, her eyes popped open as she reached to grab it back. He held the vibrator, still buzzing and quivering, out of her reach. "One of the things that makes sex even better is control of your body." He thumbed the switch and the buzzing stopped. "When you learn that, you earn the pleasure of coming."

He bent, gathered all the toys, and placed them back in the bag. She lay there astounded and hovering on the edge of climax. Her hand went back to her pussy.

"Don't even think of making yourself come until I give you permission."

She stared up at him. From her position on the floor, he loomed tall, dark and severe. Her chest rose and fell with her frustrated breaths. She wanted him, needed him. "Adrian…" she begged.

"Get up. Clean yourself and come into the living room."

"But…"

"Would you rather the training room?" he asked pleasantly.

She scrambled to her feet. No, not the training room. Still dazed and frustrated, she stumbled into the bathroom and under the shower. What had she let herself in for? He'd let her, no demanded, she make herself all hot and ready, and then he'd denied her!

Surely Kendra hadn't suffered this way. She took her time, soaping and rinsing repeatedly as if she could wash away both her frustrated cravings and her humiliation. At last, though, she turned off the water and dried herself.

He waited at the dining room table for her. There was only one place setting, but it was set beautifully, with an ecru lace placemat, a matching linen napkin, and shining silverware. A crystal goblet held iced water with a slice of lemon, and on the silver-rimmed china, a salad of greens and fresh vegetables made her mouth water. A tiny silver cup held dressing.

He rose and held the chair for her. Surprised by this courtesy, she seated herself and reached for the napkin. "Aren't you eating?"

"I'll have my lunch later. You may eat."

When she picked up the dressing to pour it over her salad, he said, "Only half."

There wasn't much in that thimble, but she did as instructed, then picked up her fork and took the first bite. The greens were fresh and tender, the vegetables crisp, the dressing delicious.

"Take small bites," he ordered. "Chew each one thoroughly. Make each mouthful count."

She savored every bite under his approving eye, until there were only a few lettuce leaves left on the plate.

"Leave those," he said.

"But I'm still hungry."

"Moderation, Norris. Moderation. Control your hunger. Discipline your body."

Discipline. She hated that word. Gritting her teeth, she put down her fork.

"Drink your water."

She enjoyed every cool drop, deliberately lingering at the table. He'd surprised her with a nice lunch when she'd expected to starve. He surprised her again when he held the chair for her to rise.

He ushered her into the middle of the room. "I'm going to leave you now to think about a few things."

She nodded, looking forward to stretching out on the lazy couch for a nice nap.

"Assume the position."

Since she was growing used to doing that whenever he entered or left, she thought nothing of it. She sank into the kneeling position on the soft, deeply padded carpet. This time, however, he had her place her hands behind her back and before she could yank her hands away, had slipped something over her wrists and up her arms.

"These are leather sleeves," he said in a conversational voice. "They will help you keep this position. Shoulders back," he instructed and pulled on the sleeves, bringing her wrists close together and securing them so she couldn't move her arms.

"Now, wait just a moment," she began, but stopped abruptly when he placed a gag over her mouth. She pushed at it with her tongue, but he fastened it securely. She began to scoot away from him, a useless maneuver when he grabbed her ankles and tied them together, wrapping something about her knees so that she was immobilized.

She raised pleading eyes to him.

"Now, Norris, I'm going to leave you. While I'm gone, I want you to think about your reasons for being here. Think what you want to accomplish. Ask yourself if fighting me every step of the way is worth it. Ask yourself if you have what it takes to learn discipline to achieve your goals."

He turned off the light as he left, leaving her in total darkness. She tried to sit back on her heels and couldn't. She tried to loosen her bonds and couldn't. She tried to scoot forward and couldn't.

She could only kneel there where he'd left her, trussed and silent. Crying didn't help since she couldn't breathe and cry at the same time.

She didn't know how long she'd been there, getting increasingly disoriented in the dark. She had nothing to rest against, nothing to ground her. Her shoulders throbbed with the strain of holding them back so far. Her legs cramped. The feeling left her toes.

Eventually, she toppled over and gasped as she hit the floor. The gag loosened a bit, allowing her to breathe easier. She rested there, forcing herself to calm down, and as she did so, Adrian's instructions came to mind.

She did as he said, thought about her reasons for being there, her goals, and her commitment to losing weight and getting sexy.

Much as she hated to admit she'd been stubborn or even wrong, Norris remembered Kendra doubting that she could control her temper to follow the program. She didn't want to prove her right.

More than anything, she wanted to prove to herself that she could do it. And that meant listening to her inner voice counseling her to follow directions, absorb all the punishment Adrian handed out and show him that she did indeed have what it took.

She'd show him.

Chapter Five

She roused when Adrian slipped off her restraints. He rubbed her arms and legs until circulation was restored. Ignoring her moans and groans, he stretched a large towel on the floor, then rolled her onto it, face down.

The sweet fragrance of oil drifted past the pain and teased her senses. She murmured deep in her throat as he worked out the knots in her shoulders and smoothed his hands away from her spine. This was more like it. Every little nerve ending, in every inch of skin he touched, whimpered in pain, then murmured in pleasure. Relaxation eased along her body, leaving her limp and drowsy.

At last, too soon, he ended the massage and stood. He wiped his hands and capped the bottle of oil. "Have you thought about your goals?"

With an effort, she rolled to her knees. Placing her palms as he liked them, she nodded. "I'm ready to get with the program."

"That's good. You're a stubborn woman, Norris. If you put that to work for you, there's no reason why you can't leave here with everything you want."

"I'd like that."

"On your feet. It's time to go back to work."

She hauled herself to her feet and followed him into the training room. She paused in the doorway, waiting for him to tell her what to do. He gestured to the middle of the floor.

She sank into position and waited quietly while he adjusted the padded weight bench. Strange, her knees didn't hurt as much as they had before, and even the strained muscles of her arms and calves didn't ache. The man had magic hands. She wondered how they'd feel if he was using them to make love? Imagining the feel of them on her breasts, stroking her pussy, and cupping her ass sent a warm glow through her. She recognized it as arousal, and was pleased with herself. When Adrian did get around to having sex with her, it wouldn't be as bad as she'd feared. In fact, she was beginning to look forward to it.

She wondered what he did in his off hours. Did he have a girlfriend, or heavens… "Are you married?" she blurted.

He looked up from his task. "Did you ask permission to speak?"

She blinked at his severe tone. They'd been talking so freely before she'd forgotten his stricture against talking. "I forgot. I'm sorry."

He studied her face, as if checking her sincerity. He nodded.

She placed her finger against her mouth as he'd instructed. When he nodded again, giving her permission to speak, she asked, "Well, are you?"

"No. No more questions."

Well, thank goodness. It was bizarre enough being naked all the time with a male trainer, but if he was married, arousing her, making her talk about sex and teaching her improved techniques, that would be too weird!

She couldn't help wonder where he got his own sexual expertise. With his looks, he was sure to have women after him. She thought about his other clients. Maybe he was the reason they came for refresher courses. Maybe they couldn't get enough of him. Her stomach clenched as she thought of him with other women. She couldn't be jealous, she reassured herself. She had no reason to be envious of his experiences with other women, but still, the thought of Adrian and other women made her uncomfortable.

"Lie down here." He gestured at the table he'd set up at his waist level. She climbed up and stretched out as he positioned her, flat on her back with her knees bent. She expected him to hand her some weights and wasn't sure she could even lift one, not the boneless way she felt, but instead, he took one hand and secured it to the side, then did the same with the other hand.

When she made no protest, he raised an eyebrow. "Very good. You're learning."

His words warmed her. In a daze of self-congratulations, she didn't protest when he placed her feet in stirrups and secured them in place. Ordinarily she hated being in this position at her doctor's and never hesitated to say so, but now she lay quiescent, only mildly curious about his intentions. She watched him as he scooted the chair closer and sat between her spread feet. Her pussy was fully exposed to him.

"A woman's body is a mystery to a man," he murmured. "A man is never sure what a woman is feeling unless she's in the throes of climax, and even that isn't a sure thing. Too many women fake it. Do you, Norris?"

"Sometimes."

"Why?"

She looked down her body at him. He looked interested, as if he really wanted to know. She liked him like this, when he watched her with curiosity and his eyes intent and warm on hers. He half-smiled, encouraging her to be open and honest. Open she already was, but she had to dig into herself for the honesty. It was hard to shrug when she was tied down, but she managed to move her shoulders. "Sometimes because I just want it to be over."

He nodded. "You're not enjoying it. Is that because of you or your partner?"

"I don't know. Could be either one. Something isn't right."

"What if you were in control of the situation, and could make sure that you get every bit of pleasure out of sex?"

She had to laugh at that. "Dream on."

He reached out and flicked her clitoris. She yelped.

"Today we are going to practice simple lessons in self-control, Norris. I am going to show you what a lover should do. You are going to accept everything, tell me what you like, what turns you on. You are going to learn about your body, experience pleasure, but..." He drew out that word, making her squirm in anticipation.

"But what?" she dared ask.

"I will not allow you to climax."

"Why not? It just happens!"

"No. You may not have an orgasm until I permit it. That will be your reward for controlling your responses."

"What if I can't stop it?"

"Then you will learn the penalty for your lack of control." He pinned her with his eyes as he said this, making sure she understood the penalty would not be pleasant.

"But…this isn't how I usually make love."

"We are not making love, Norris."

She stared. "But you said… I mean, I thought you and I were going to—"

"Have sex?" he supplied. "No. We are not going to do that."

"But you promised." She heard the disappointment in her words and clamped her lips shut.

"I promised to teach you how to make love. How to get the most out of it. How to satisfy yourself and your partner."

She hesitated, trying to recall his exact words. He'd said something about techniques. Greater pleasure. How could he do that without actually having sex with her? Her brow creased.

He saw her confusion. "Good sex begins in the mind," he instructed her. "Thinking about it. Being aware of your lover. Anticipating what will happen." He looked at her, making sure she understood.

"I know that." She was anticipating right now. Her skin felt hot, her insides opening. Moisture gathered between her legs and her breasts felt fuller. She couldn't touch them, but she could feel her nipples tightening.

"Good sex is also physical stimulus and response. Some responses are involuntary, like your body preparing itself for sex. Temperature changes, lubricity, nipples swelling, like they are doing now." He touched one and she shivered.

"Those you can't control. But some you can. You can control your body's responses. Having control over those things increases the experience. Prolonging the experience means a more satisfactory orgasm."

"You mean mind-blowing sex."

"Exactly." He seemed to fight a grin. He firmed his mouth, but the humor touched his eyes and for an instant, the heat from them flowed over her like warm chocolate. She grinned back, sharing the moment with him.

Grin under control, he gestured at the restraints. "Those will restrict involuntary movement so you can concentrate on learning control."

She swallowed.

He reached forward and tapped her nipple. "Normally, a man doesn't touch a woman's breasts until he's aroused her. Kisses and strokes and close body contact usually go first. Think about that for a minute. Can you imagine that happening now?"

She wasn't sure. Many of her sexual experiences had involved some groping, and the steward had kissed and suckled her breasts, but he'd spent more time pumping into her. She closed her eyes, imagining Jack Rodriguez touching her, his lips on hers, tongue busy in her mouth, his hands stroking and cupping her breasts, his fingers plucking at her nipples.

It didn't work, she kept losing her place, forgetting what he was supposed to be doing. Maybe because Jack had never given her a second look, not lustfully, anyway, that she couldn't picture him. Instead, his face kept morphing into Adrian's. It was Adrian's long fingers she saw at her breast, his mouth closing around the nipple, his tongue flicking it until it popped up. Just as it actually did. And it felt so good!

She made a little sound, not quite a moan. She opened her eyes, to see Adrian watching her carefully. "Tell me what you were thinking." His hand cupped her breast.

She moistened her lips as heat spread across her chest and up her neck. "Someone, a man, touching me."

"How?"

She told him, carefully omitting the tiny little detail that it was he who turned her on. With each word, her insides warmed, until her breasts fell hot and too full.

He released her breast and ran his finger down her belly. She hated that it quivered under his touch but she couldn't deny she liked the way it made her feel.

"Tell me," he demanded.

She licked her lips. "Hot and soft and liquid bubbling inside."

"And this?" His finger probed her curls.

"Impatient. It's not enough." Her breath came faster as she tried to hide her response from him, but he saw. His eyes narrowed as he gauged her reaction and varied his touches. He circled the curls on her mound, traced the junction between thigh and belly, and tickled her belly button. Her breath came faster.

"You are responsive, Norris. That is good. A man likes to know he can arouse his woman." His eyes caught and held hers. "Now tell me what else you feel."

"Shivery. Like hot, like cold. Like all my senses are focused on one place..." She closed her eyes against his demanding gaze. She held on to the sensations of his finger against her sensitized flesh, making this delicious anticipation last. She forgot her hands and her feet secured in the stirrups. All feeling was concentrated in her abdomen, in the warm pulse arrowing down to her clit.

His finger stilled. She could feel the heat of his hand, poised just above her skin. She held her breath, waiting for him to touch her again.

"Norris."

The air cooled her skin. *Oh, no, don't stop!* She opened her eyes.

"I don't like to be kept waiting."

"Neither do I," she muttered. She waited for him to touch her intimately.

"What do you feel?" he asked again.

She blew out a breath. "What you want me to feel," she retorted, frustrated that he'd stopped touching her, angry with herself for being so easily manipulated and eager for him to put his hands on her. "Hot, antsy. Touch me!"

He stood and withdrew a step. "Are you in control of your body right now?"

She pulled against the strap on her wrist. "How can I be?"

"Settle down. Take a deep breath." When she'd done so, he sat again, looking carefully at her exposed pussy.

She cringed. It was one thing to have him look at her while he touched her, another thing to be on display.

"We'll start over. This time, enjoy the sensations, tell me what they are, and hold on to each one as long as you can."

She studied his face between her legs. Perspiration beaded his upper lip. His mouth was closed tight. What did he have to sweat about? She was the one on the hot seat.

"Now." He repeated his earlier actions, reaching between her upraised knees to touch her, wait for her response and touch her again. In slow motion, driving her crazy. She searched for the words to describe her response. "Excited. Sensitive. Oh…do that again."

He complied.

"Antsy. Focused." She tried to control her breathing, but it quickened along with her pulse. "I can't take much more of this," she all but whimpered.

"You'll take as much as I want to give you."

"It's too much."

"Hardly." He sat motionless, only his eyes monitoring her involuntary movement. She felt twitchy, hot, unfulfilled.

She panted. Swallowed to moisten her dry mouth. "Please," she pleaded.

"Please what?"

"Touch me again."

When he did, her hips rose automatically. "Be still," he commanded.

His finger delved through her curls, then unerringly circled her bud. Rather than touching her clit, he followed the curve of one of her pussy lips down, then the other one up.

She squirmed. Empty. Longing. Gradually, a sense of place and time returned to her. This was so cold, trussed up, immobile while he toyed with her, emotionless. She stared at his face, looking for some indication of his feelings.

Found none.

He showed no signs of interest in her as a female, only in her as a lab specimen. That hurt. Humiliated her. This was awful. Demeaning. Her throat squeezed shut and she bit her lip to stop the tears welling up behind her eyelids.

"Stop," she whispered.

Instead, he circled her bud again, butterfly touches that brought heat to her clit. It felt so good. So terrible!

"Stop," she cried.

He flicked her clit in reprimand. Without a word, he continued arousing her with strokes, tickles and teasing. She couldn't take any more.

Her eyelids felt heavy but she forced them open. Stared at him in disbelief. Now his face was drawn, his cheekbones pronounced and his mouth a tight grimace. If arousing her was so distasteful to him, why did he keep doing it?

What did he get out of working here? Pervert! Forcing women to submit, then playing with them like objects. Where was the satisfaction in that?

And, *ohmigod!* It felt so good. What he was doing to her made all her senses come alive. Made her focus solely on the little nubbin of flesh between her legs. With only one finger he had her so aroused she couldn't see straight, couldn't think, couldn't do anything but feel. He hadn't even touched her inside and she was so close. So close! Nothing mattered but his finger on her clit. She clenched her muscles.

He raised his eyes to her face. Now she noted the beads of sweat on his upper lip and on his forehead. The room was warm in consideration of her nakedness, but not that warm. His breath came faster. He had to be feeling something, too, but whatever the feeling, it was lost in her own personal need.

She moaned, twisting away from his touch, lifting her hips to get closer, begging for more. Begging for release.

"Not until I tell you to come," he reminded her. His voice was raw.

She panted, her inner muscles working like vises with nothing to clamp around. She wanted, she wanted, oh oh oh, she wanted him! She needed him, his finger, his cock, something inside her. She needed it *now*!

She was desperate for him, desperate to climax. "Please, please."

"Control it. Control your body," he commanded harshly.

"I can't," she cried, all but sobbing with her need. Her hips lifted in invitation. "Please!"

"Not yet." He was firm, resolute, absolutely unyielding.

She bit her lip. She clenched her fists. She tossed her head from side to side, but she held on. The aching between her legs rose through her body, gnawed at her breasts and burned her throat. She held on. She whimpered, she sobbed, she cried, but she held on.

"I'm going to count backward from ten to one. When I get to one, I'll let you come."

"Oh," she panted. "Count fast!"

"Ten."

She squeezed her pussy muscles tighter, tight as she could with her knees spread wide.

"Nine."

She tasted blood on her lip. Her inner muscles clenched.

"Eight."

Her juices flowed more copiously.

"Seven."

She couldn't hold on any longer. She came, in a great gushing release.

Adrian withdrew. He crossed his arms over his chest and looked at her. Such a cold expression, even with the sweat on his forehead. She panted, gazing at him half-blind, sweating herself.

"We have a lot of work to do yet," he said at last. He undid her restraints. "Clean yourself."

With effort, she got herself off the table. Her knees gave way. She grasped the table for support, then realized Adrian's arm was around her waist, propping her up. She could feel his strength in his hardened arm muscles, feel the pounding of his heart against her temple. As she gained her balance, she noted the trembling in his arm, his rock-hard torso and his hurried breathing. She felt his chin rest for a moment on her head and his chest expand as he drew in a large gulp of air. His hand tightened on her hip. Was that a caress or did she imagine his palm sliding over her butt? He released her slowly. "Go."

She stumbled away from him. Still reeling from her orgasm, she made it across her suite and into her shower. She turned on the water and stood under the multiple showerheads pounding her with warm water. Her body felt drained, weakened both by her climax and anxiety. She'd failed. Even though she'd imagined a softer side of Adrian during her test, and felt him shake when it was over, she knew he wasn't pleased with her. Somehow she knew he'd keep at her until he was satisfied with her control and reaction.

What torment would Adrian come up with now?

He hadn't told her how much time she could take, or what to do next. She soaped and shampooed as fast as she could, then dried off quickly and went back to the training room.

He wasn't there.

Chapter Six

She didn't know what to do. Should she assume the position and wait for him? She was exhausted, her body crying for rest, but if she stretched out on her bed and fell asleep, would he discipline her?

She paced from windowless wall to windowless wall. Her world was silent, empty without Adrian. Where was he?

Tiptoeing, she walked to the door of her suite. She hadn't been out of her rooms for days. She put her ear to the door, and hearing nothing, opened it just wide enough to peek out.

There was no one in the hall. The other doors were closed. The silence unnerved her. For all she knew, she could be the only one on this floor. She wavered, half in and half out of her suite. Curiosity about the other rooms edged her forward. Caution moved her back.

In a made-for-TV movie, this was when the heroine would sneak down the hallway and out the door. Or smack into whatever monstrous evil lurked in the darkness. She wasn't stupid. Adrian wasn't evil. Just unbelievably controlled and self-disciplined. As he wanted her to be.

Feeling silly, she closed her door. She'd determined to do whatever it took to reach her goal, to leave here slim, sexy and in control of her own life. Somehow she'd find the strength to follow the program, do all her exercises, eat properly, and learn to command her own body. And while she was doing all that, she'd concentrate on Jack who didn't know it yet, but he was in for the greatest sex of his life.

Norris sank down onto the plump cushions of the couch. Ordinarily, she'd have settled back into her favorite position, half sprawling, half sitting, but now it didn't feel right. It was too comfy. Without a second thought, she slipped off the couch and knelt, assuming the position.

She gazed down at her opened palms. She'd never learned to read palms, had no idea what the lines meant, but she knew her life was her own making. It was up to her to decide what she wanted to do with it.

And strangely, now she wanted to make Adrian proud of her. Whatever he demanded of her, she'd do her best to deliver.

With that resolve uppermost in her mind, she barely heard the door open. She heard a man's laugh, then realized it was Adrian, talking with someone outside her suite. His laugh was warm, vibrant and infectious. She liked the sound of it, and yearned to hear it directed at her. Why didn't he ever laugh with her? She'd love to share a joke with him, find out if they had anything in common besides the client/trainer relationship. The laughter stopped as Adrian closed and locked the door behind him. She didn't look up, even when his black boots came into view.

"Very good," he murmured. She kept her head down as warmth crept through her, making her heart beat faster.

"As a reward, you won't have to ask for permission to speak."

As a reward, it sounded better than it actually was, since she'd broken that rule countless times. Funny, he hadn't castigated her for that very often. Still, as a symbol that he thought she was doing better, that was good. Very good. "Thank you."

"Stand."

She got to her feet, vaguely aware that it wasn't as difficult. She flicked a glance at him, noting that he had bathed and changed, too. His face was freshly shaven, still stark and severely handsome. He wore a black jumpsuit, emphasizing his lean physique. Looking at him, and seeing no trace of his earlier reaction to her sensual ordeal, she almost imagined she'd seen it. But she had. He hadn't been able to do all that to her without feeling something himself. He might act like a robotron, but underneath, he was a man. One she wanted to know better. She smiled and wondered what he looked like naked. She'd bet he'd be amazing.

"You've shown me you are responsive. Foreplay doesn't seem to be a problem. That means that whatever issues you've had with sex in the past haven't been caused by any lack on your part." He nodded at her relieved grin, his expression pleasant. Her smile grew wider. "But you have trouble with control, Norris. Part of that is normal, particularly physical response to pleasurable stimuli, but it is something you can learn."

Her smile fell apart. How cold it sounded when he put it like that. Mind-numbing sex as pleasurable stimuli? Just the thought of how he'd made her come with just his finger on her clit made her nipples pop.

He circled one. Her nipple grew. Heat spread through her chest.

"You'll enjoy your body much more when you respect it. Teach yourself discipline and enjoy the physical rewards."

Familiar words, but it was hard to concentrate on anything but the tip of his warm finger against her skin. Heat on heat. She glanced up and saw that his gaze was fixed on her breast. She looked for a sign that he was affected by what he was doing. She saw none. "Do you get off doing that?"

He ignored her question, but not the sensations he was arousing in her. She looked closer, and could now tell by his intent gaze, the hardening of his muscles under his clothes, that he wasn't as immune to physical reactions as he would have her believe. His eyes barely open, his mouth thinned as his finger traced up her throat, to where her pulse hopped and skipped, then down to circle her breast and down past her belly to her mound.

Her breathing quickened. The nerves under her skin along his path jumped to attention. She took a deep breath, steadying herself, as she stood quietly under his exploring finger. He explored the curls of her mound, then down between her legs. Their eyes locked together. She said nothing, could say nothing, as she waited for him to touch her clit. To penetrate her. Anything!

Instead he pulled back. She made a little sound of distress, then clamped her lips together.

"Go run a tub and get in it."

She blinked. She'd just bathed.

"Now."

She hurried into the bathroom. Once again she wished there were some bath salts or fragrant oils to dump into the water. When she'd registered for the spa, she'd expected all those luxuries, not spartan soap and shampoo, and she wanted them now, to be fragrant and soft for him.

She ran the water as hot as she could stand it, then climbed in, sinking to her chin in the steaming water. It felt so good to give herself up to the soothing heat. Her eyes drifted shut.

"Don't go to sleep in there."

She opened her eyes as Adrian entered the bathroom carrying a small black case. She licked her lips, nervously wondering what was in the case, but she didn't have long to wait.

He opened it and propped it on the edge of the tub. Inside, a gleaming straight razor, a shaving brush, a leather strop and a shaving cup with a bar of soap, nestled in individual compartments. She raised her eyes to his. "I shaved this morning."

"Those disposable razors aren't enough," he murmured as he rolled up his sleeves, revealing muscled forearms. He dipped the shaving cup into the tub and scooped up a small amount of water. As she watched, fascinated and yet somehow fearful, he made up a lather then set the cup aside.

He stropped the razor and tested it with the edge of his thumb. Nodding, he set that aside, too. "Lift your arm."

She lifted her arm and held it as he indicated. She watched as he lathered her armpit with the brush and flinched when he applied the razor. He had a firm, smooth touch, placing the sharp blade against her skin, then moving it down skillfully and quickly. That wasn't so bad. He rinsed it, then repeated the action, shaving her without comment. Apparently without any interest other than making sure he left her skin smooth and uncut.

"Other arm."

She had to turn around in the tub. While he waited for her, he stropped the razor again. Once she lifted her arm, he shaved her armpit with the same silent care.

"Leg."

She was used to the routine now, even if it did seem unnecessary. She could tell this was a closer, smoother shave, but why bother? She asked the question.

"I want you smooth," was all he'd say. He shaved one calf, then the other.

"Stand up."

She did, splashing water on both of them. He gave her a warning look, then applied himself to his task. It wasn't bad, she thought, having someone else do all the work. In fact, she could almost enjoy it, enjoy the way he touched her skin, holding her in place, then running his palm over it to check for any missed spots. She wound up facing away from him, bracing herself on the cool tiles above the tub.

He stropped the razor and made up more lather. "Spread your legs."

Instinctively, she closed her thighs.

Without warning, she felt a stinging lash across her wet, bare bottom. She whirled, making waves in the water, and saw the strop in his hand. "You hit me!"

"Spread your legs."

Incredulous, she eyed the strop in one hand, the razor in the other. "You hit me," she repeated and rubbed her butt. A welt ran across both cheeks. "That's abuse."

"That's discipline." He looked at her squarely. "You gave your permission."

He had her there. She might not have known to what extent access to her body meant when she signed the agreement, but she'd done it. "Don't hit me again."

"Do as you're told, then."

She opened her legs.

"Lift your foot." He placed her foot on the edge of the tub, and applied the lathered brush to her mound. The soft bristles tickled and she couldn't help contracting her muscles. He glanced up at her and she made herself stand still, even as she asked, "Why are you doing this?"

"You have a full bush. To some men, that may be a turn-on, but I need to see you."

Oh.

With care, he lathered her up and shaved her. She glanced down and saw her brown curls dropping into the water. All right, so that wasn't so bad.

"Spread wider."

Her eyes widened instead. He was going to use that razor on her pussy? She glanced up, saw his face implacable and stern.

Swallowing, she widened her stance. The brush was awful, teasing her and arousing her with each soft swirl. By the time he picked up the razor, she couldn't stop a whimper.

"Be very still."

The first touch of the steel against her tender pussy lips brought every bit of her focus on that tiny strip of skin. He took his time, using short strokes, ultra-careful, shaving every last hair. She held her breath when the blade circled her clit, then closed her eyes at the exquisite sensation of the blade slipping over her sensitized skin. Every glide of the steel awakened new nerve endings, promising pleasure. Her breathing grew short as she held herself still, all senses concentrating on his touch on newly bared skin. Her pussy lips closed, then opened, inviting him in. She shivered when he ran his fingers over her flesh, checking his work.

At last, ages later, he rinsed the razor and dried it. She exhaled. He replaced each item of the shaving gear in the case, then looked at her. "You can rinse off now. When you're finished, go to the training room."

Oh no…

She did as she was told, washing away every bit of lather, every bit of arousal. When she walked naked into the training room, he was seated in his armchair waiting for her.

He looked comfortable while she was a walking case of nerves. What did he have in mind for her now? He didn't make her wait long after she dropped to her knees in front of him. "Time for exercise."

Given her choice of exercising or a swat on the butt, she'd take the swat. Grumbling under her breath, she moved to the mat.

He led her through her stretches, then her exercises, seeming to delight in each groan and moan. When she'd stop at ten repetitions, he took her to twenty. When she flagged, he spurred her on.

After a break for water, he took her through another set. Even at her gym, with machines to do the work, she'd hated working out. Having to do it all herself was unendurable, but endure it she did, until at last, Adrian led her through her cool down routine. She collapsed, face down on the mat.

"Slightly better," he said. "By the time your stay is over, this will be a breeze."

Oh ha-ha. She could only think it. Speaking was too much effort.

"Now that you're rested, come over here."

She pulled herself upright and saw what Adrian meant. She flinched. Not that table again! She dragged herself over to it and climbed up.

"On your belly."

She rolled over. He pulled her arms over her head and placed them in restraints. She shivered but didn't protest, not even when he nudged her legs apart and secured her ankles to either side of the bench. He left the table. She waited, afraid to breathe, for his next move.

When it came, she all but groaned with delight. He poured a pool of warm, scented oil in the small of her back, then massaged her from head to toe, applying a firm, no-nonsense stroke that had her sore muscles screaming, first in pain, then in delight. The fragrance of almond drifted in the air around them. Drenched in pleasure, she sighed deeply. This was more like it.

He kneaded her butt cheeks. "Have you ever had anal sex?"

She tensed, remembering how a long-ago lover, sure she'd love his big cock rammed up her ass, had forced her to it. "It hurts."

"Not if you're prepared. Not if it's done right."

"It's dirty."

"Not when you take precautions."

"It doesn't feel good," she said at last, desperately.

"That's where you're wrong. Did you know the anus is ringed with sensitive nerve endings?" He rimmed her with a lubricated fingertip as he spoke. "Feel that? Hundreds of them."

"Aah…"

"See? When your partner takes the time to prepare you, you might enjoy it." He paused, while she tried to imagine that. "We are going to find out."

He slipped the tip of his finger in her. "The skin here is soft, like satin, and hot."

She squirmed, tensing against the pain she knew was coming. His finger withdrew. She heard him move away. She looked over her shoulder at him, and saw he'd opened the spa's bag. She knew what was in there. Those dildos…

He brought the set of three to the table and held them where she could see them. "These are anal dildos. Probes. Some people call them butt plugs. They come in many sizes and shapes, but we'll begin with these three. The smallest," he said as he pulled it from the case, "is the one we'll start with. We'll work up to the larger sizes."

She swallowed, once, twice. He sounded so prosaic, so ordinary, as if this was no different than brushing his teeth. "I'm not sure I'm ready for this."

"Who is in charge here?"

"You are," she said without hesitation. But could she trust him not to hurt her?

As if answering her unspoken doubts, he said, "The object is not to inflict pain, but to widen you gradually." As he spoke, he uncapped a tube of lubricant and spread it liberally over the small probe. Then he took more and applied it to her ass, between the cheeks and into her anus. "That should do it."

He patted her butt cheek. Norris took comfort from it. Then with one hand, Adrian spread her crack wider and slipped the tip of the dildo in. She tensed. "Just relax, Norris. This isn't any bigger than my finger and you took that."

She swallowed the knot in her throat and unclenched her muscles.

"There. That's the way. Good girl."

The unexpected compliment sent warmth flooding through her. She relaxed, feeling eased and pleased, and without her aware of it, he'd inserted the dildo in as far as it could go.

"See, no problem. Now," he flicked the switch and the tiny dildo buzzed. "What do you feel?"

"Ooh," was all she could say.

He kept the dildo in her butt, turning it, edging it in and out while she closed her eyes and let him give her pleasure.

Abruptly, the buzzing stopped. He pulled the dildo out. She moaned in protest.

"Quiet."

She glanced over her shoulder at him and saw that he was lubricating the middle-sized dildo. Her eyes widened as she realized how much wider and longer it was than the first one. Instinctively, she made a small noise of protest.

He smacked her rump. "Control, Norris." He applied more lubricant to her ass and inserted the tip of the dildo. She felt the pressure as her inner walls were pushed apart. She whimpered but he continued inexorably. Her breathing quickened. It wasn't pain she felt, just a newness, an unaccustomed sensation that had her heart racing and her pulse jumping.

When he turned the dildo on, the vibrations shuddered up her spine, down her arms, around to her breasts and shot unerringly to her pussy. She cried out, not in pain, but in arousal.

His hand delved under her. His fingers found her clit, pulled it. She gasped at the touch of his finger on her denuded pussy and felt her inner muscles clench. With the dildo in her ass and his fingers busy beneath her, she concentrated on the pleasure spreading through her body. It rushed through her veins, heating them, pooled in her abdomen, making her juices flow freely, then trickled through down to her toes, making them curl.

"When I get to one, you may come," he instructed, his voice uneven. "Ten."

She panted.

"Nine."

She tried to close her legs against the sensations flooding her.

"Eight."

Heat shot through her, scalding every inch of her. The vibrations buzzed in her head, in her bones. She tossed her head from side to side, as if that would release the pressure escalating within her.

"Seven."

Her fists clenched. "Oh, please, let me…"

"Six. Focus!"

Her butt was on fire. Her pussy screamed for something to fill it.

"Fi—"

Her orgasm hit her like a blast furnace. She came in a great gust of scorching heat. Her body shook with it, her inner muscles clenching and clasping. She yelled with the pleasure pain of her muscles clamping on the dildo in her ass.

Adrian turned it off and pulled it out. In the sudden silence, she could hear him breathing. Harsh and hurried, as though he too was close to climax. Though she was face down and couldn't see him, she felt him close to her, felt his heat enveloping her, almost as though he cradled her in a lover's embrace.

"Better," he panted. "But not good."

Not good? Any better, and she'd die from the pleasure.

Days later, when she'd lost count of time, Norris ended her sets on the cardiovascular equipment. She panted, pleased with herself. As Adrian had promised her, the exercises were getting easier, and as much as she hated to admit it, she did feel better for doing them. More energetic and strangely enough, calmer.

"Clean up. Put on a tunic and wait for me."

A tunic? After days of being naked 24/7, putting on a tunic was an event. She hurried through her shower, soaping and shaving, keeping herself clean and smooth as he preferred. She realized she primped for him as she would a lover, not just the dragon who trained her body and every day demanded increasingly more of her.

She hesitated at the choice of tunic, all in ocean colors, aqua, navy, sea foam and white. She slipped the turquoise tunic, as the one most flattering to her coloring, over her head and entered the living room.

He stood near the door, dressed again in his usual black, but today he wore a tank top that revealed the muscles in his shoulders and arms and his flat abs. He was lean, tall and mouthwatering. Norris swallowed. It was getting harder to act as though he meant nothing to her, as if he was only an employee at the spa who performed his duties well. She waited impatiently for him to come to her suite in the morning, and felt deprived when he left. It was impossible to deny that he turned her on without even touching her. With just the sound of his voice, the scent of his skin, the warmth of his body.

And aroused as he made her, it was doubly impossible to deny she wanted him. Hard to fly apart at his touch and not demand full-bodied sex.

He looked her over as she approached and knelt at his feet. "Good. You may stand."

He opened the door and led her down the hall. She hadn't even looked out since the day she'd peeked and felt a little strange, like a stranger journeying down new paths. How silly! It was just relief at getting out of her rooms after being cooped up day after day.

He stopped in front of the same door she'd been in before. He gestured her in. "I'll be back shortly."

Angela waited for her. "Hi. It's good to see you again. We're going to check your progress."

Norris joined her behind the curtain and stepped on the scale. *Ohmigod*, was that right? She stepped off the scale and on again. It was right. She'd lost nine pounds!

Angela smiled and jotted the numbers in her file. Next, she took some of the same measurements taken on Norris' first day here. "You're doing very well. You're developing more muscle mass."

Norris grinned. "I've been developing muscles I never even knew I had."

Angela frowned. "You don't want to overdo it. Does Adrian know you're doing that?"

"He's right there, watching me." And pushing her, forcing her to feel more, experience more, give more.

"Sounds like you are getting along with him?"

"Could be better," Norris said. It would be much better if she could get Adrian naked and doing her more intimate exercises with her.

"Well, keep up the good work."

Pleased with herself, Norris couldn't stand still while she waited for Adrian. She paced and broke into an impromptu tap dance.

Adrian's laugh stopped her. She whirled around. When he laughed, his smile spread over his face and up into his eyes. They were a warm chocolate, and with his laugh, they made her think of hot fudge. But she wasn't hungry for candy or sweets.

"Don't stop on my account," he said, still smiling. "You're pleased with the results?"

"Nine pounds!"

He took the file from Angela and studied the notations. He nodded at her and she left the room. He turned to Norris. "Very good. You've earned a reward. What would you like?"

Chapter Seven

You! The thought popped into her head. Ordinarily, her first reaction would be to think of something yummy, gooey and delicious to eat. Something to fill her mouth.

She still wanted to fill her mouth, wanted something delicious, but all she craved now was Adrian. His taste, his flesh. His cock.

"An hour of television?" he suggested.

A few days ago she'd have jumped at the idea of meeting other clients, of tuning in to a news channel, finding out what was going on in the world. She shook her head, no.

"A chocolate truffle for dessert?"

She hesitated. "No."

He smiled, rewarding her. "I'll think of something."

Her mouth went dry.

He gestured at the door and took her back to her suite. As soon as he'd locked and closed the door behind them, she whipped the tunic off and sank into her submissive position.

"Very good, Norris."

Praise from Adrian was rare and doubly valued. She let it sink in, spreading warm feelings throughout her body. With Adrian's approval, who needed chocolate?

He sank down into an easy chair, propped one knee over the other and studied her file. He made an entry or two, then studied her. "You've made a good start on the basics. You've surprised me. I didn't think you'd last this long, but here you are. Ready to go to the next step?"

Her eyes widened. What more was there to do? She exercised, ate right. She was losing weight. Cautiously, she nodded.

"You don't seem very sure of yourself." He paused, as if waiting for her reassurance. "No matter. Go into the training room."

She got to her feet, more easily now, she noted and walked away from him. Pleased with her changing body, she walked shoulders back, spine straight, enjoying the sway of her breasts.

He followed. "On the table, on your back."

Obediently, she climbed up and stretched out. Her hands rested on her hips, then crossed over her belly. She noted with pleasure that it was just a bit flatter. She could find her hipbones. Smiling, she waited while Adrian went to the armoire and returned with the bag of toys. Teaching instruments, as he called them. Hah.

Wide-eyed, she waited. A bit uneasy, a bit excited. What this time? He didn't make her wait long, as he opened the smallest box and took out the Ben Wa balls. He held them up so she could see them. "Have you used these before?"

"No." She'd heard people talk about the balls, how they made women hot in a matter of minutes, but didn't believe them.

"They'll help you learn to control your vaginal muscle. The PC muscle. The more you control that muscle, the better your orgasms will be."

How could they get any better?

"Today we'll find out how you respond to them." Adrian held them in his hand, then tossed them from hand to hand. She thought she heard a small clink as they fell into his open palm. "Raise your knees," he instructed. He looked at her pussy, then dipped his finger in a jar of lubricant.

He smeared the lube over the entrance to her pussy lips, avoiding her clit, until they opened of their own accord.

He nodded then inserted a finger, then two, spreading her open. When he was satisfied, he took the silver Ben Wa balls and pushed them up into her. They were cold, and she shivered. Apart from an alien item in her private parts, she felt nothing. Fat lot of good these things did. Adrian shoved them a little higher, then tugged a bit on the string, making sure he could remove them, she guessed.

She waited. Nothing. She flicked him a glance, noted his watching expression and shrugged. "I don't feel a thing."

"You will. Get up and walk around."

She hopped off the table. Moved. Walked a few paces. And stopped. Oh wow. Those little buggers were doing their job. The vibrations as they rocked together and against the walls of her pussy got stronger with every step.

She darted a look over her shoulder at Adrian. He nodded, a slight smile on his face. "Get on the treadmill."

She felt her eyes widen but she did as instructed. He set the pace at the lowest and turned the machine on. She took one step, then another, and another. Oh double wow. The Ben Wa balls inside her moved with each step, pushing against her inner walls, creating friction, creating heat.

"Oh, I had no idea," she gasped.

"Keep walking." He increased the pace a little and she walked faster. The heat inside her surged, melting her insides. She could feel the balls caressing every sensitive bit of her. Places inside her she'd never thought much about were coming to life, caressed and cajoled into pleasure. The sensations grew and grew.

Adrian kept a close eye on her responses, watching her pulse beat frenetically in her throat, her heart clang in her chest, her knees wobble. Still, he gave her more.

"Adrian, I can't…"

"Keep going. Contract your muscles. Hold them in."

She breathed harder, panting now. Sweat popped out on her forehead, dripped down her face to her bare breasts. She thought the drops would sizzle on the burning flesh there.

"Take them out!"

"Walk." He checked the monitor. "You're doing fine. From now on, you'll use the balls at least once a day. I'll insert them, or teach you how, but at least fifteen minutes a day."

Nodding, she walked. And walked some more. She began to writhe, her upper body twisting and turning to escape the increasingly unbearable pleasure of the metal balls inside her. Her juices escaped her and trickled down her thighs. She moaned, she cried. And walked.

Abruptly, Adrian lifted her off the machine and carried her to the table. She tossed from side to side, almost falling, until he spread open her legs and yanked on the ribbon.

The balls came tumbling out, and with them, she exploded into a great gushing orgasm. Her body shook as the spasms took her. Adrian planted a hand on her belly to keep her from rolling off the table. The heat of his hand added to her pleasure, tumbling her again into sensation. She cried out with her release. Gradually, in minute stages, her body slowed. She rested, panting, as sensations ebbed and left her immobile, helpless against the vast pleasure/pain she'd just experienced.

Gradually, she became aware of Adrian still at the foot of the table between her legs. She focused on his face, his expression drawn, his gaze intent on her pussy as his hand slowly moved over her still quivering belly to her pussy. His touch caressed and soothed. His mouth was closed tightly, his breathing harsh. Anyone would think he was in pain as he ran the tip of his finger around her engorged pussy lips. He blew out his breath, then found a towel and wiped her dry.

"You did better than I expected." His voice was calm, matter-of-fact, but Norris heard his approval. She managed a smile, which he returned. In full measure. It was the first time she'd seen him smile like that, naturally, warmly. It felt wonderful to be on the receiving end, to feel an emotional connection with Adrian.

She lay still, perfectly happy to do nothing but wallow in fading physical sensation. Her pulse slowed, resuming normal pace while Adrian took care of her. He allowed her to rest for some moments, while he sat in his chair. He put his head back, staring at the rod across the ceiling and taking several deep breaths. If she didn't know his iron will, she'd have thought him holding on to his own control with effort.

She watched him eye the rod, fearful that she'd disappointed him somehow and would wind up suspended like a slab of meat again.

He rubbed his jaw and sat up. "Go shower."

She pulled herself upright and on rubbery legs made it to the bathroom. This time, she didn't care how long she took as she lathered and rinsed. The heat of the water dissolved any bit of remaining starch in her bones and she slid down to sit on the tiled floor, water cascading over her head and shoulders.

Who would have thought those little metal balls could have such a huge impact?

"Norris?"

She lifted her head and peered through the steam. Adrian's figure was a dark blur beyond the glass enclosure. "Yes?"

"Are you all right?"

A different kind of pleasure speared her. It was the first time he'd asked that question. It took her a moment to control her happiness. "I'll be out in a minute. I'm fine."

He moved out of sight without a word, but when she pulled herself up and turned off the water, he was there with a warmed towel. He dried her from head to toe, then walked her to her bed.

He'd already pulled the covers back. "Take a nap." His voice was softer, almost tender.

Gratefully, she crawled in and collapsed against the cool sheets. Adrian pulled the covers over her shoulders. "I'll wake you later."

Later came much too soon. She forced an eye open as Adrian shook her shoulder. "Up."

She groaned and rolled over.

He pulled the covers from her. "Up. Now."

She groaned again but pulled herself to a sitting position. Her body felt spineless still, muscles robbed of all strength. "I'm so tired."

"Three minutes to the training room." His voice had lost all tenderness. He spoke briskly, as cold as if he'd never displayed any tenderness or concern for her. She'd basked in his care of her and now he acted as if it had never happened.

She watched him leave her bedroom without a backward look. Resentment stirred. How dare he be so untouched by what he'd put her through? She muttered to herself but resentment wasn't enough to keep her from following orders. After a brief stop in the bathroom, she made it to the training room to see Adrian looking at his watch.

"I'm still tired."

He eyed her. "So you're tired. So what? Control, Norris. Self-denial."

She controlled the words that wanted to spew forth. She denied herself the pleasure of venting her anger. Instead, she smiled as sweetly as she could and dropped to her knees.

He chuckled. "Very good, Norris."

She kept her head lowered and her face hidden, afraid he'd see her uncontrolled reaction to his praise.

"You worked hard today. In fact, you lasted longer with the balls than I thought you would. You had a good orgasm?"

He sounded so detached! How could he ask that as if it mattered no more than a pleasant walk in the park? Not that she ever walked in the park, of course. "It was very nice," she responded, her voice as cool as his.

He chuckled again. Those brief, infrequent spurts of humor were positively luring her in. "Good. As a reward, you can have the rest of the day off. Think about what you've accomplished so far. Think about what you've got ahead of you."

He turned and left her suite. For this he woke her up? Grumbling, she got to her feet and walked back into her living room.

What was she to do with the rest of the day without Adrian?

* * * * *

The next morning, bored silly by having nothing to do but work out and sleep, Norris was thrilled to see Adrian enter her suite and lock the door behind him. She slipped into her submissive pose with a smile on her face.

He didn't smile back.

Instead, he put her through her exercise routine, adding extra sets and extra weight. She counted, breathing in, breathing out, maintaining her posture. When he ended the session, she drank her water and waited while he readjusted the weight bench.

She watched, enjoying the sight of his muscles moving under his T-shirt and loose sweatpants. It wasn't hard to admire his body or his concentration. She wondered what he had in mind for her today. He gestured. "On your belly."

Oh, please, not the butt plugs. She should be wide enough by now, session after session. She hesitated a little too long.

"Do I have to repeat myself?"

He made sure she didn't like it when he had to repeat himself. She clambered onto the table and stretched out face down.

"Today we are going to see how well you do on your own. I'm giving you the chance to control your body, but if you can't, I'll use the restraints. Clear?"

"Yes," she mumbled.

"Lift your hips." He slid a cushion under her, lifting her bottom higher. He patted her butt cheek, then traced his finger down between the cheeks, circled her anus, and dipped lower.

He tested the smoothness of her labia, murmuring praise when he found her freshly shaven. She expected him to fondle her clit, as he usually did, but instead, he plunged a finger into her.

She wasn't ready for that. She was dry, and it hurt. She yelped. Instantly, he withdrew his finger and flicked her clit. She yelped again, then held herself very still, waiting for his punishment. It wasn't long in coming. She felt the air move first, then his hand landed on her bottom in a swift, hard smack.

"Ouch!" she cried. The smack was hard enough, but it was shame that she'd lost control that hurt. She felt the heat on her bottom cheek.

"Quiet." He ran his palm over the hot spot. She could almost imagine it as a caress, soothing away the small pain. He lifted his hand, and she tensed, not knowing whether she should expect another blow.

His finger was back a moment later, this time lubricated and penetrating her gently. She relaxed. His finger circled inside her, massaging the walls of her pussy, making her feel good. Her nipples grew and pressed against the bench as her belly heated.

He stopped. She knew better than to protest or ask for more, and waited for what he would do next. She glanced over her shoulder and saw him lubricating the middle-sized dildo. He inserted it, gently, steadily, praising her when she remained still.

He worked it in to the end, then withdrew it, back in and out, while he played with her clit. Her juices flooded his hand.

"Very good, Norris. Your arousal rate keeps getting better and better. We just need to work on prolonging it." While he spoke, he withdrew both his finger and the dildo. In a moment, she felt him applying more lube, then holding the tip of something else to her ass. She closed her eyes, knowing it was the largest of the three butt plugs. He hadn't used it on her yet, and she'd known that one day he'd make her take it. Apparently, this was the day. She willed herself to be calm, to show him she could take whatever he wanted to give her.

As before, he lubed her, and slowly, gently inserted the dildo, allowing her to adjust gradually to the larger size. He was patient with her but where other times he'd played with her pussy and caressed her clit to make it easier for her, this time, he forced her to concentrate only on what he was doing to her ass. She grabbed at the table to hold herself still.

He murmured something under his breath. Norris strained to make out the words and couldn't but felt encouraged by his tone. He sounded like he was praising her, or even as if he was describing how her skin felt.

Deeper, deeper, deeper. He pushed the dildo in until Norris felt she could take no more, and then pushed it in again. She felt spread open, totally exposed, nothing hidden from him, taking what he put in her to please him. *Please him*? She froze at the thought. Everything she'd done up to now had been to please him, to lose weight and enhance her sexuality according to his program. What was so different about this time?

It was hard to think with sensations from the butt plug taking over everything in her body, but she held on to the question until, with the last shove that seated the dildo completely and fully in her ass, she knew the answer. She wanted Adrian to see her as a woman, not as just another client to take through the paces.

She wanted him to want her as much as she wanted him.

Dimly, she heard him speaking. "…did very well. We'll just leave this here a moment and let you get used to it."

She relaxed, aware of her body on the table. Her breasts felt full and heavy. Her belly ached for something to fill her pussy as thoroughly as the plug filled her ass. She loosened her grip on the table, realizing only now how hard she had held on. Her ass felt on fire, stretched and throbbing with the intrusion of the large dildo, but it felt good, too. Adrian had tested her, and she had passed.

A few moments later, how many she didn't know, she felt his hands on her butt cheeks. He smoothed the flesh away from her anus and then slowly pulled the dildo out of her. She gasped as it left her. Her ass felt empty, yet the slide of the dildo against the nerve endings Adrian had sensitized made her yearn for more. He rimmed her anus with his finger and she moaned with pleasure.

She waited for his instructions. He said nothing, but soon she felt something cool against her pussy lips. Still enveloped in the pleasurable haze, she turned her head to see what he was doing. When he saw her looking, he raised his hand so she could see what he held.

The double pronged pussy and ass dildo. *Oh, no!* She'd been dreading this, dreading how it would feel to be penetrated both places at once, dreading both the pain and the pleasure. The dildos were long and thick. The pussy one was wider than anything she'd ever had before. She'd never be able to take it!

"Please, no…"

"Yes, Norris."

He inserted the tip of the vibrator in her pussy, but didn't turn it on. As he had with the dildos, he played with her, getting her used to the wider girth, inserting it a bit deeper each time he withdrew and plunged it into her until most of the dildo was in her. She felt her pussy walls expanding under the pressure, astounding her as she took more and more of the huge dildo. The other tip poised at her ass. Her breathing quickened. Anticipating, dreading, wondering, oh please…

He flicked the vibrator in her pussy and turned it on. Instant pleasure oscillated through her veins. She moaned, and barely felt the tip of the smaller, curved vibrator push through her anal muscles. Adrian set up a slow, rhythmic thrust and counterthrust, in and out, opening her, penetrating her, both orifices at once.

She moaned. Oh, she'd dreaded it, but oh, oh…it was so good! Her knees shook but she gripped the table and held on.

He turned on the vibrator in her ass. The double vibrations jerked her neck back. *Ohmigod, it was so good!* She felt every buzz from the top of her skull to her toes curling under. She floated on an engulfing sea of sensation, focusing on nothing but the mounting heat in her belly, the craving, the desire, the feel of hundreds of sensitive nerve endings caressed at the same time. He breasts were so full, the nipples pressed painfully flat against the bench. She panted.

"Ten."

Oh, she'd never make it to one.

"Nine."

Please please please…

"Eight."

She screamed.

"Seven."

She gripped the table harder, crying now.

"Six."

Her muscles couldn't take it. They clenched and gripped.

"Five."

She lost track of everything but holding on.

"Four."

Pleasure drenched her. *Aahhh*, her muscles convulsed. Screaming she couldn't take any more, she quivered and trembled and came so hard she couldn't see. It went on and on, so hard and so long her body felt battered and bruised. The main climax ended, leaving her twitching with aftershocks, each one less, dissolving, until she lay drained.

She didn't move, not a twitch, not a muscle. Spent, thinking was out of the question, but gradually, oh so slowly, she became aware of something that wasn't quite right. Something missing.

She'd had another stunning climax, and she should have been sated, out of her mind with release. Not this time. It wasn't the physical sensations that were lacking. God, no.

Her body couldn't take any additional onslaught and thought was difficult when all she wanted to do was rest, but something nibbled at the edge of her awareness. It wouldn't let her be until she recognized it. Physically and mentally, she felt glutted, but emotionally, there was something lacking. She wanted more. As satisfied and surfeited as her body was, her spirit felt empty, Deprived. She didn't want to be only the receiving end of pleasure. She wanted to share it, to give it to Adrian.

Her labored breathing slowly evened out. She felt the wetness on her cheek before she knew she was crying. Wiping her tears away took too much effort.

She felt Adrian remove the dildos. After the intensity, the heat of them in her body, she felt cool and empty. She was drained, exhausted and somehow, very lonely. Such an intense physical sensation, such far-reaching pleasure was too much for one person alone. It had to be shared.

He straightened her legs, took the pillow from under her hips and tucked it under her head. She accepted his comforting gestures as she did everything else he did to her body. She just wished there was something personal in his actions, some tiny hint of tenderness he'd shown her earlier.

She craved his recognition of her as a person, as Norris Brownell, not just a body to put through its paces and see how much it could take. She wanted him to accept and acknowledge that she, Norris Brownell, had an affect on him, too. On Adrian...she didn't even know his last name!

It wasn't enough to get a glimpse, every now and then, of the way he reacted to the torments he put her through. Getting sweaty himself or breathing hard might make her think he was aroused by what he did to her, but she wanted more, damn it. She wanted him to admit that she turned him on, too. That he wanted her as she wanted him. As a man wants a woman.

He left her for a few minutes and came back with a warm cloth and a light blanket. He wiped her clean, then covered her. The room was warm, but the soft weight of the blanket made her feel secure, cared for and very tired. She murmured her thanks.

He scooted the chair around to the head of the bench. "Don't go to sleep, Norris."

Chapter Eight

She forced her eyes open. His face was almost on a level with hers. His usual composed and distant expression was gone. Instead, he looked strained. Frazzled. Not at all like someone who was happy with his work. It made her feel fractionally better. "You're doing well. Getting more control of your body, but—"

"Can't this wait?"

"You can nap later. Pay attention."

She sighed. "What?"

"You've come as far as you can—"

She giggled.

"No pun intended. Listen." He waited while she struggled to focus on him. "You've proved you can take physical stimulus and hold off, to a certain degree," he added with a stern look, "finding your release."

She basked in his limited praise.

"But."

Wasn't there always a but? What did he want from her now? How much more could she take?

"But your response and control is with mechanical help. How you will you do with an actual partner?"

The image of Jack Rodriguez flashed through her mind, then disappeared. The reality of Adrian, sitting so close to her that she could feel his warm, minty breath on her face, was overpowering. She knew his touch in every orifice, she knew his manly aroma, she knew his sexual expertise, but she didn't know him. Not intimately. Oh, as often and as thoroughly as he'd touched her, bathed her, massaged her, poked his fingers in her, all that was done impersonally. Not as Adrian the man touching Norris the woman.

And that's what she yearned for. She ached to feel him in her, his hot cock buried as deeply as he could go, longed to see his passion etched on his features. She wanted to hold him in her arms, before, during and after sex, ached for him to fall apart in her arms. Yearned to fall apart in his.

That's what was missing. No matter how hard, how long, or how completely he made her come with those devastating orgasms, it wasn't enough. It wasn't flesh on flesh, heat on heat, body slamming into body with only one desire burning though skin and bones down to the intimate core. It wasn't personal.

"Norris," he asked in a voice so calm it belied the expression on his face, "what will you do when a man makes love to you?"

She'd shatter. She moistened her lips. "I don't know."

"Don't lie to me."

"I mean it. I don't know."

He studied her face. God, she must look worse than a cat's leftovers. She'd cried, which meant her eyes were red and swollen. Her lips were cracked. Her tongue felt twice its size, her nose hurt from pressing it into the bench. She'd tossed her head about. Her hair must be a mess. She wanted Adrian to see her as a desirable woman, not a pitiful, crying lump.

"Do you have a lover waiting for you?"

She thought of Jack. "No."

"Any commitments?"

How pitiful she must sound. "No."

"Single and free, then."

She flicked a glance at him. His expression had evened out, but it was slightly different. He was still austere, but was that a smile on his face? Was he laughing at her?

"Do you remember our conversation about improving your sex life?"

"Yes." It was hard to get the word past her dry throat.

"Have we been doing that?"

"Yes. No."

"Which is it?"

"Anyone can play with bedroom toys."

His eyes warmed. "So they're not enough?"

"Not always," she hedged.

"What more do you want?"

Was he going to make her ask him? She looked down at the floor.

"What more do you want?" he repeated in a no-nonsense voice.

It helped not to see his face when she answered. "I want the real thing."

"Sex with a man?"

She nodded.

"With whom?"

She flicked a glance at him, then at the floor again. "You," she mumbled.

"Speak clearly."

She glared at him. "All right, dammit, with you! Now, are you happy?"

He chuckled, damn him. "You want to have sex with me?"

Did he need it spelled out? She wanted to make love, not have sex. She didn't want any more tests to see how long she could last. She wanted to explode with him inside her and feel him do the same. "You know I do."

"Maybe."

She looked up at him, curious. Did he mean…?

"If you earn it."

"Earn it." She echoed, her spirits falling. "How?"

"By pleasing me. "

"Haven't I already done everything you said? You said you were pleased with my progress." She heard the incipient whine in her voice and stopped. Controlling her tone, she asked, "What more is there?"

"You'll see."

She could hardly wait for the chance to do whatever he wanted of her. It wasn't easy, but her spirits got a boost when she entered her bathroom for her evening shower and found her reward.

Bath oil, a loofah and fragrant skin conditioner were lined up on her bathroom counter with a single white rose in a dark blue vase.

She skipped the shower, ran a full tub and squirted in bath oil with a free hand. She eased into the hot water, sighing with pleasure and rested her head against the edge of the tub. Her body was slimmer, her senses sated. Idly, she cupped her breasts, then pinched her nipples, thinking of Adrian and his hands on her. She slipped one hand down her flattened belly, and between her legs. With a soft stroke, her clit popped out and she circled it, recalling Adrian's fingers caressing her, penetrating her, making her experience every pleasurable sensation. And he'd promised her sex, real one-on-one sex.

Did life get any better?

It got worse.

She didn't know what more she could to do please Adrian. She did her exercises as well and as enthusiastically as she could. She ate when and where and what he told her. She slept and bathed when he told her. She spoke only when he allowed her to. She dropped another six pounds, losing a total of almost half of her goal. What more could she do?

He'd stopped testing her sexually. He rarely touched her, even accidentally. No more opening herself to him and taking whatever stimulus he wanted her to feel.

She'd felt degraded even as her body convulsed with pleasure, but now she missed it. Missed the daily, sometimes two or three times daily that he'd taken her to the edge, demanded she teeter there, then shot her over. She missed his touch on her breasts, her pussy and even her ass. She was hungry.

He'd taken all the bedroom toys, including the Ben Wa balls that she'd gotten used to using while exercising. She found that out when she'd awakened late one night in a fever. She'd touched herself with her fingers, but that wasn't enough. She wanted penetration, deep and hard. She'd climbed out of bed and gone into the training room but the drawer where he'd stored the bag of toys was empty. She'd searched the entire room and come away disappointed.

And feeling empty. Frustrated. She wanted sex, wanted the hot spiraling increase of tension, the heated release. Damn it, she wanted Adrian.

He'd promised. She'd agreed. Why wasn't he coming through for her? Well, she reminded herself reluctantly, not exactly promised. He'd said *maybe*, but that meant he could or would. Instead of showing her he was at least thinking about having sex, making love with her, he'd backed off.

He observed her weight training, watched her technique and nodded approval. She finished the last set with the weights and put them to one side. She inhaled, then caught his eye. "I...I thought we were going to have sex."

"Have you earned it?"

"What more can I do?" she asked, her voice almost breaking. "I've done everything you asked."

"And done it well, too."

She stopped, taken aback by his praise. Warmth seeped through her veins, and she grinned. "I have, haven't I?"

He grinned back.

Oh, what that grin did to his face. If he was attractive before, that smile devastated her. She wanted to taste it, taste him. Put her mouth on him and take his tongue into her mouth. Suckle him...

"Then why—"

He lifted a finger. She stopped speaking.

"Very good, Norris. I didn't think you had it in you, but you're learning control. I'm pleased with your progress."

His words were better than a fat contract with an even fatter fee. They zinged through her, spreading satisfaction and a sense of wellbeing throughout her body. Her shoulders went back, her spine straightened. Her breasts lifted.

"Thank you." Such simple words to tell him how much his approval meant to her. "So, can we…" she drifted silent, embarrassed that he was making her ask again.

"You want this?"

Her mouth went dry. Did she want him? Did the dawn follow the night? She nodded.

"In words."

"Yes."

He waited, all the while watching her face. He must have read desire, humiliation, her want. His eyes narrowed.

"Yes. I want to make love."

"I can see that." He shifted his stance, widening his legs.

She stared at his groin. She'd wondered so often what his penis looked like. Was it long, broad, cut? Now she was going to find out! She waited for him to make a move.

A moment passed, then another and another. "Um…"

"You have to earn your reward," he stated.

She lifted confused eyes to his face. "My reward?"

"Lose another ten pounds."

"That's not fair!" she burst out. "You keep changing the rules!"

"Is that so?"

"I've done everything you asked. Let you touch me any way you want. Now you want me to wait?" she wailed.

He lifted an eyebrow in silent reprimand. Norris wasn't listening. "You've pushed me and punished me and made my life a living hell and I won't take it anymore!"

"Really?"

She was so angry she shook. "Who the hell do you think you are? Some king or pasha with a slave girl you can dominate and treat anyway you want?"

He gestured at the door. "If you care to break your contract, be my guest."

She glared at him. Oh, she was tempted! She'd been here long enough to make new exercise and eating habits. She could walk right out that door now and keep right on doing her exercises and eating sensibly and lose the rest of the weight on her own.

She could justify what she'd learned so far, and the new habits she'd made, as worth the exorbitant fees. Breaking the contract meant she forfeited the rest of her money, and she was still bound to maintain the spa's confidentiality, but maybe it was worth it. She'd get out of this place and go find Jack and she'd seduce him and…

No, she couldn't. She blew out a long, pent-up breath. She wasn't going to quit. She'd proved she could get this far. She was so close now to her goals that she could stick it out a little longer. She was positive about that. She just wasn't as sure she could bear being with Adrian and not having him. "You've been jerking my chain," she said at last. "I have a right to be treated with respect."

"Correct. Respect your body and it will respect you. Earn respect from others."

"What has that got to do with making love?"

"Stupid question. Without it, sex is meaningless."

"But…all those dildos and vibrators, making me wait to come, that's not respect for me as person."

He eyed her for a long moment. "Quite right. Sometimes you have to break down the barriers, destroy all the old habits before you can begin to build new ones. Teaching you your limits, taking you to those limits, and then beyond, well, consider that breaking down the old so you can start over."

"Ridiculous!"

"Are you the same person you were when you entered *Sweet Discipline*?"

"No-o."

"Of course you aren't. You're in better shape, physically and mentally. You're acquiring control, replacing bad habits with better ones."

She nodded. "Okay, so that much is true. But teasing me, arousing me, then backing off, that's cruel."

"If you say so. Or," he paused and challenged her, "you can look at it as an incentive. Lose those pounds and we'll have sex."

She felt like throwing something at him. "I don't want to wait!"

"Too bad."

She advanced on him, close enough to feel his breath on her upturned face. "You can't tell me you haven't gotten aroused, too."

His eyes turned heavy. "No comment."

"I've seen you. I can tell when you're holding yourself back."

"Control is important."

She edged closer, her naked breasts whispering against his shirt. "You wanted me. Don't you want me now?"

He swallowed. She watched the movement of his throat, then flicked a glance up. Perspiration beaded his upper lip. She lifted her hand and ran a finger down his jaw, then his throat.

He caught her hand in his before it reached his chest. "None of that."

"Is it because I'm still fat?"

He held her hand for a moment before releasing it. "You are still over desired weight, but that's not the reason. Your body is womanly, with curves in all the right places."

He walked around her. "You can't see it yet, but I can." He ran his hand down her arm. "Your muscles are taking on definition. You're building muscle where you were flab."

He traced a finger around her middle. "You're getting your waist back. Your hips are smaller." He tapped her abdomen. "Your belly is shrinking." He ran his hand over her ass. "Your butt is firmer. Many men will find your body type arousing, an earth mother reaction."

"How about you?" she whispered, humiliated to find herself responding to his touch. More than responding, going soft and liquid.

"My interests are not in question here."

Damn! Why couldn't he give her just a little of himself? He knew all there was to know about her, all the intimate, embarrassing details. Why couldn't he reveal something about himself?

She drew on her inner strength. "So, if I'm not fat, what's the reason you won't make love—have sex with me?"

He eyed her coolly. "It's against company policy for one thing."

"Then why did you say we would?" She challenged him openly, not at all submissive or deferential.

He looked her straight in the eye. She knew she wouldn't like what was coming.

"You needed the incentive."

She didn't like it. She felt betrayed, like a child promised a treat and then having it snatched away. "You lied to me. I hate liars."

"Hate me if you want. Clients often do."

She hated being lumped in with other clients. She wanted to be special to him. "Do you promise to have sex with all your other clients?"

His mouth twitched, as though he repressed a smile. "I'm not going to answer that. Confidentiality and all that." His smile broke through. "Would you want me telling other clients about you and your arousal rate?"

She glared at him. "Stop laughing at me. I've tried my hardest and I've lived up to my part of this deal. So when are you going to live up to your part?"

"Are we back to the sex or are you talking about getting you in shape?"

"You know I mean the sex!"

He walked away from her. At the door, he stopped, turned and looked her over from head to foot. She couldn't decipher his expression, but her spirits rose. He came back. "If I decide to make love to you, you'll be the first to know. If we have sex, it will be private, just between us."

Aha. Maybe she had something going here. "So if I rat you out, you'll get in trouble with the management?" She grinned. "With the dragon lady?"

He laughed. "She is, isn't she?"

"What's the second thing?"

He looked taken aback.

"You said company policy was the first thing. So what's the second?"

He crossed his arms over his chest. "That's personal," he said through thinned lips.

She snorted inelegantly. "And all those things you've been doing to me weren't personal?"

He shook his head. "If the client wants them. You did."

Oh, he had an answer for everything. She turned her back on him and walked away, half expecting him to order her back.

He did nothing of the sort.

She stepped on the treadmill and switched it on. She started slowly, warming up with a gentle pace. Ignoring him. He came to stand at her side, watching her technique.

He nodded. "Good. I'll leave you to it."

She turned her head and watched him leave. That was it? He was walking away after getting her all primed. She exhaled loudly, then turned back. Let him leave. She had better things to do than fuss about his reasons for backing away.

Company policy, my ass. He was as turned on as I was.

Upping the pace, she strode, then ran and ran. Her breath came fast as she sweated away the miles. Sweated away the desire that gnawed on her insides.

When she was too tired to run anymore, she slowed, stepped off the machine and wasn't surprised to find her legs rubbery. A shower helped.

She stretched out on her bed. It was deeply comfortable and she'd slept better here than anywhere else, but now, though she was exhausted, her bones crying out for rest, her mind wouldn't slow down.

How long had she been here? How many days to go? Apart from the kinkier aspects of her stay, she couldn't fault the program. She placed her hand on her stomach. It was flatter. She could even feel a dip where before there had been a definite bulge. She smiled and checked her hipbones. There they were, all right.

She had more endurance, less flab on her arms and legs. Her muscles were toning. She didn't want the bodybuilder look, that's for sure, but she could live with a sleekly toned body. Live with? Hah. She craved it.

She wanted to walk into a room and own it. She wanted admiring looks for her body as much as she wanted respect for her mind and intelligence.

Intelligence. That was the key. She'd use her smarts to make the best of her stay here. Screw Adrian and his hot and cold nature. She'd clear her mind, concentrate on her physique, build her stamina and lose the weight. Never mind what Adrian had promised her when she lost the next ten pounds.

She wouldn't have sex with him if he had the last working penis on earth.

Chapter Nine

As if he knew of her decisions and respected them, Adrian kept their sessions over the following days simple and to the point. He worked her hard, forcing her to go a little bit more each day, making her reach deeper within herself to go one more set, one more step.

He didn't touch her. He studied her body, noting her progress with the detachment she now welcomed. They spoke only when necessary, and he no longer supervised her mealtimes. She had it easy here, with excellent meals prepared and served without her having to lift a finger. It was effortless to eat what was on her plate, and even leave a few bites of her chocolate mousse. She couldn't remember when she'd last had a craving for candy.

Adrian would be proud of her, but he wasn't here to see.

He started leaving her alone for varying periods of time. At first that was difficult to get used to, accustomed as she was to his presence, but then she began to look forward to being by herself.

At least, when he wasn't present, she could stop trying so hard to be as distant and professional as he was. She could stop not looking at him, stop wondering for the zillionth time what he looked like naked, wondering how his muscles bunched and released during a workout.

She could stop fantasizing about making love to him. Correction: having sex with him until neither of them could walk.

Instead, she wondered what he did when he wasn't with her. What did he do when he left her for the night? Where did her live and what did he do for fun? Did he live alone?

Did he have a girlfriend, a lover? She scowled. Had he been getting all worked up arousing her and then going home and satisfying his passion with another woman? Or was he gay? Was that why he could touch her and not want her? Did he take his superlative body home and share it with another man? What was he thinking of when he used the butt dildos on her?

Jealous. That's what she was. Jealous because her trainer might be getting it off with someone else. She gritted her teeth and closed her eyes, trying to block out the image of Adrian pumping into a faceless person. Her chest ached, her nipples felt bruised. She had no right, no reason to feel this way, but it felt like betrayal.

The thought scoured her insides, turning the taste of sweet mousse to bitter bile.

She left the table, knowing someone, faceless and efficient, would clear it while she was in the training room. She began her afternoon session with the weights, proud of herself from having graduated from the puny two-pounders to the heftier ones. Up and down, breathe in and out.

She'd moved on to her abs work when Adrian entered the room. Immediately, she stopped what she was doing and sank into the position.

He nodded absently, then walked around the room, checking the equipment as he did daily. He had an abstracted expression on his face, as if something bothered him.

Norris was proud of herself. Normally, she'd wonder what upset him and be peeking at him from her downturned eyes. Today, she was distant, contained, in admirable control of herself. Should Adrian notice, he'd only see her looking calm and serene.

He wouldn't see how her insides fluttered.

Adrian circled the room, touching this, examining that. He pulled out drawers of the cabinet, checking the contents. He looked distracted, and some of that spilled over onto her.

She fidgeted.

"Be still," he snapped, in the severe voice she hadn't heard in days.

She subsided, but she watched. His hair looked messy, as if he'd run his hands through it. His clothes, his usual black jumpsuit, looked rumpled.

He paced another circle, then slumped into the chair. It was the first time she'd seen him sprawl, his shoulders down and head sunk forward. He looked like a man with a lot on his mind and none of it good. She watched him warily. He wouldn't be in here, acting like he'd just lost his last friend, if it didn't involve her.

He hadn't had to discipline her lately, and even when he had felt it necessary to correct her, he'd handled it easily, in control, showing no emotion. It made her feel unbalanced, uneasy, and uncertain.

He lifted his head and stared at her. His face, always severe, was etched with something she couldn't quite identify. Worry? Fear? Anger? That was it. Anger. He was pissed about something. With her? What had she done? She racked her brain and found nothing. She began to tremble. Whatever it was, this wasn't going to be fun.

He cleared his throat. "Something's come up." He frowned. "I mean, there's something I need to tell you."

She swallowed. "Have I done something wrong?"

"No, it's not you. Well, it involves you, but you're not at fault."

She'd never seen him at a loss for words. It made her restless and fearful in return. Relieved that he wasn't incensed with her, but how else could she be involved?

He stood abruptly and began to pace. She turned her head, keeping her eyes on him as he prowled the room. He stopped before her.

"Stand up."

She scrambled to her feet and waited anxiously. Her heart raced.

"I'm going to turn you over to another trainer," he stated.

An immediate sense of loss swept through her. Her eyes widened. "Why?"

His narrowed as he stared at her. They were a deep, dark brown, richer than the most scrumptious chocolate. She lost herself looking into them. Almost mesmerized, she couldn't look away. "Why?" she repeated in a whisper.

He swallowed. "I've lost my objectivity."

"What do you mean?"

"Just what I said. Another trainer can get you back on track."

"I wasn't aware I was off track," she whispered. "I've done everything you tell me." Her voice gained strength. "I'm losing weight. Getting control."

He nodded.

"Then why?" She thought fast. "You said no other trainers were available."

"They weren't then. One is now."

"I don't want to start over with another trainer. I've gotten used to you." Now *that* was an understatement.

"You can get used to someone else," he answered roughly.

"But I don't want someone else." She reached out to him, touching his chest. "I want you."

"Damn it." He reached for her, swept her into his arms, and kissed her. His mouth was hard, punishing, and desperate.

She was too startled to react at first. His heat enveloped her, surrounding her with his power. She stiffened. She'd been very much aware of his body before, but not like this. Pressed close to hers. His height, the breadth of his shoulders and the strength of his arms held her contained while he devoured her mouth. She'd wanted his kiss, but not like this. She tried to break away, and couldn't break the vise he held her in.

Then gradually, as his grip eased and his mouth softened, she responded. His lips brushed hers, once, twice, as if apologizing for the rough treatment, then coaxing, teasing, inducing her to open her mouth to him.

She felt trampled. Conflicting emotions and feelings ran over her roughshod. She couldn't sort out her reactions, couldn't believe he was kissing her, couldn't believe the about-face. And then she didn't care anymore why he was kissing her. It was enough that he was.

She kissed him back. She opened her mouth to him, pulled him in and gave him anything and everything he wanted while she feasted.

She explored his mouth, savoring his taste and his tongue exploring hers. This was what she'd craved, his body pressed so close to hers she could hardly breathe. The heat and strength of him drawing her into his spell. The taste, *ohmigod*, the taste of him, dark, powerful, commanding and demanding.

Her knees buckled under her. His arm caught her and held her upright while a hand swept up her naked curves and cupped her breast.

He had touched her before, aroused her before, but never like this. Fevered, frantic and fabulous. Holding nothing back.

Abruptly, he let her go. His breathing was harsh, as harsh as the angles of his face. "That's why."

She stumbled and grabbed the back of a chair to hold her upright. Still unsteady on her feet, she panted, trying desperately to get her own breathing under control. "Yes, yes. Let's do it, right now."

"No."

She whirled away, blood rushing to her face, then turned to face him, her anger running hot and deep. "How can you do this to me? To us? I know you want me. I tasted it just now! You want it as much as I do!"

"Maybe more," he admitted, his chest heaving. "Do you think it's been easy, arousing you, making you come, seeing how good it is for you and not being able to do anything about it?"

"But you can! I want it. You want it. Why stop?"

"I'm not going to have sex with you," he said harshly, his voice as rough as the look in his eyes.

"But I want you!" she cried, sexual frustration making her voice sharp and needy.

"I want you, too," he admitted. "Too damn much."

"Then why...?"

"Because it wouldn't be sex. That I could handle. Making love, I can't."

He turned on his heel and was out the door before she could say anything.

She stared after him, her mouth agape.

Chapter Ten

Norris heard the door open and automatically dropped to her knees.

"What are you doing on the floor?"

She glanced up. A woman dressed in a hot pink sports bra and black spandex shorts stood in the doorway.

"Who are you? Where's Adrian?"

"I'm Rachel, taking over for him." She flicked an assessing glance over Norris. "Get up, get some clothes on. Wear your sweats."

Norris scrambled to her feet, embarrassed and angry. She didn't want another trainer, especially a skinny little thing who flaunted her toothpick body in skimpy workout clothes.

She took her time, deliberately dawdling as she pulled on clothes. They felt strange against her skin, now that she was used to being nude all the time.

Rachel waited for her, seated in the armchair Adrian had favored. Norris frowned.

"Adrian has his training techniques," Rachel said in response to her unvoiced question. "I have mine. I won't require any of the methods he's been using."

Norris nodded, thankful for that. If she'd found it difficult and humiliating with him, it would be doubly so with a woman trainer. Still, she felt unsure. She'd gotten used to and felt comfortable with the deference Adrian required. It gave her limits and incentives. What was she supposed to do now? Should she stand or sit?

Rachel answered her unanswered question by waving her to a chair. Norris perched on the edge of it.

"I see why Adrian wanted to switch. Don't worry. It happens with all his female clients."

Norris stopped short. All his clients? She was no more than another body to him?

Rachel studied her face, then sighed. "Have you heard of the Stockholm syndrome?"

Of course she had. "Kidnap victims getting attached to their kidnappers, forgetting other relationships."

"Something like that."

"You're suggesting that's what happened between Adrian and me?" Norris asked, not hiding her scorn. "Forget that."

Rachel eyed her dubiously. "Granted you aren't a kidnap victim, but when you see only one person, rely on that person in a situation like this, it gets pretty intense."

Rachel had a point, Norris acknowledged. "Not for a moment have I forgotten who I am or my life outside this place." She made her voice firm and absolute.

"It's easy for a woman client to fixate on a male trainer." Rachel went on, ignoring Norris' protests. "She can imagine that there is more to their relationship than—"

"You can stop right there. I know exactly what there is between Adrian and me." And that's zilch, she mourned.

Rachel hesitated, then nodded. "If you say so. Adrian has his reasons, whatever they are. He's already working with another client."

Norris couldn't hide how much that hurt.

"Don't worry. You'll get over it." Rachel's voice was sympathetic, then turned brisk. "Let's see how you're doing."

She led the way into the training room and put Norris through her exercise routine. She was quick to praise and pointed out areas of improvement.

Though she didn't want to like her, Norris found Rachel's brisk, no-nonsense approach easy to work with. This was what she'd expected when she signed on, a professional coach to teach her new habits. Each training session over the next few days was better than the one before.

She knew that Rachel worked her hard, maybe harder than necessary, to help her forget Adrian, and she was grateful for the thought, even if it didn't work.

Still, when she went down the hall with Rachel for her regular weigh-in, she came back jubilant. She'd lost twenty-three pounds! She felt good. Slimmer, stronger, eager for each day.

Instead of being bored now that she was so close to her goal, she felt energized, ready to take on the world. Rewarding her efforts, little luxuries appeared in her suite. All the lotions and creams she'd expected, plus a visit to the manicurist who also gave her an excellent pedicure. She had appointments with the nutritionist, a facial to die for and a consultation with a stylist who gave her hair a new, sprightly look with highlights. She studied herself in the mirror after her session with the beautician who'd taught her some makeup tricks to bring out the green in her eyes and highlight her cheekbones. She had cheekbones!

Norris liked what she saw.

This was what she'd come here for. She was pampered, massaged, her body cosseted, and most important, she was treated respectfully. She slept deeply and well.

A few days later, she came into her living room after a session in the sauna to find a television set. Rachel saw her confusion.

"You're doing so well and will be leaving us soon. It's time to find out what's been happening in the world." She picked up the remote and switched the set on.

"No, I mean not now," Norris said quickly. She wasn't ready to make the transition, not yet.

Rachel nodded. "As you wish."

Later, that night, after her evening bath in a tub with fragrant, moisturizing oils, Norris lay in bed. She was so close to her goals and felt good about it. She'd worked hard, lost weight, slimmed down and toned her body. Her muscles were stronger. The flab was all but gone. She was in control.

Of everything but her hunger.

She didn't want food. She wanted Adrian. She craved his touch. She remembered the feel of his fingers on her breasts, her clit and her pussy. She could close her eyes and recall every detail, even the way he'd widened her and sensitized her anus, making her come so hard and so long.

Just thinking about that made her nipples pebble and her pussy go soft and liquid. She felt abandoned, bereft and betrayed. He'd promised her and reneged.

If he thought that disappearing would change the way she felt about him, he was wrong. Dead wrong.

Without thinking, her fingers found her soft spots. She caressed herself, hands skimming over her skin, still slick and moist from her bath, stroking and arousing herself as she thought about Adrian. She drifted into a fantasy in which he was the one caressing her. His fingers pulled at her nipples and wormed their way into her. She came, not in the blistering hot sizzling orgasms he'd drawn from her, but in a quiet, lonely release.

She cried herself to sleep.

When she woke, her eyes still puffy, her limbs felt leaden. A hot shower under pulsating jets revived her somewhat, but she barely nibbled at her breakfast. Lethargic and listless, she wandered over to the couch and sank down into its blissfully soft cushions. She drifted into a doze.

"Is this how you're training?"

Her eyes popped open at the familiar, severe voice. Adrian!

He stood over her, legs spread, his usual black jumpsuit making him look even taller and leaner. She felt her pulse race as she stared up at him.

"Off the couch," he ordered.

She scrambled off and dropped to her knees. Oh, it was good to have him back!

"That's better." He stepped back, eyeing her. "Stand and take off those clothes. Let me have a look at you."

She stood, forgetting how hard it had been once to get to her feet without pulling herself up on something. Now she was limber and quick, proud of her lithe body. She pulled off her sweats and dropped them at her feet.

He motioned her to turn and she did, feeling his assessing gaze on her body like an approving, tangible caress. He voiced it with a murmured, "Very good. You're looking good, Norris."

Her heart swelled. "Thank you." Those few words from him made all the days and weeks of work worth every painful moment.

He held a file folder in his hand. Now he opened it and ran his eyes down her progress chart. "You've only got a few more days with us. Looks like you'll make your goals."

"Thanks to you," she murmured.

He lifted his gaze from the page. Held her eyes with his. Deep, dark chocolate, rich with warmth and praise. Hot with need.

It was still there. That look she'd thrilled to, the one that told her he was aroused as she. She couldn't be imagining it.

"Adrian?"

"I shouldn't be here." He exhaled. "I told myself I could stay away from you."

"I'm glad you came. I missed you."

His eyes closed. When they opened, they devoured her. "I want you."

No finesse, no loving words, no compromise.

She didn't dare ask why he'd changed his mind, lest she give him the chance to change it back. Mouth dry, she nodded and went to lock the door. When she came back, she found him standing in the same spot, his eyes riveted on her.

"Make me hard."

"Wha-at?"

"You heard me."

She'd expected him to initiate sex. He'd always been the one. What was she supposed to do? "How?" she breathed.

"How do you usually do it?"

Oh, this was too embarrassing. She craved him with every inch of her body, but how could she tell him her seduction techniques sucked? "I'm not very good at this," she admitted in a small voice.

He sat in the chair, sprawling back with his legs spread. With his eyes intent on hers, he unzipped. "Any ideas?"

Ohmigod. Her pulse kicked in, raced around in circles and urged her forward. She moved slowly, settling on her knees before him. "You want me to touch you?"

His eyes went dark, hard. "Touch me? Yes. Take me in your mouth."

She edged closer, tucking herself between his knees. She bent forward, almost afraid to breathe. Hesitantly, she reached for the opening between the zipper, then stopped. Her hand rested on his thigh, feeling how his muscles immediately tensed under her shaky fingers. His cock tented the fabric over his groin.

She pulled her hand back. He was already hard.

He took her hand in his and placed it over his groin. Immediately, his cock swelled and hardened even more.

"Oh..." She looked up, saw him nod, his faint smile, and did what she had wanted to do for ages.

She explored him, her fingers tracing his length first through his clothing, then reaching in past his opened zipper to find him. He wasn't wearing shorts.

His breath hissed on a quick intake of breath when she drew him out and held his cock on the flat of her hand. *Oh, yes.* He was long, and thick, hard, with dark blue, almost purple veins that pulsed as she studied him. His skin was soft, satiny soft, covering the tempered heat. She ran her tongue over her lips. She wanted that, wanted it in the worst way.

His heat drew her. Unerringly, she curved her hand around his cock, feeling him harden even more and the pulsing growth. He didn't need her to make him hard. She already had him that way. Joy bubbled. She laughed.

"I hope you're not laughing at me. That's hard on a man's ego."

She laughed again. "I'm happy."

His smile grew, warming his face and lighting his eyes. "You can make us both very happy."

She closed her fingers around his cock and stroked.

"Aah," he murmured. "Like that."

Taking her time, she examined the marvelous creation she held. Curiosity led her to discover what he liked best, how he liked to be stroked, caressed and pleasured. She experimented with drawing the foreskin up, then sliding it back, pressing gently on the little nubbin of flesh hidden below the head. His breathing roughened, but he held himself still under her learning touch. She circled the tip, pressing a bit to make the tiny slit widen. She tapped it gently with her forefinger, lifted a tiny bead of liquid on her finger, up to her eyes.

She glanced at it, then at Adrian's face. His gaze was set on her face, expectant, the angles and planes hardened by desire.

Norris licked her lips. His eyes narrowed, dropped to her mouth, then back, encouraging her, daring her. She put the tip of her finger to her lips, flicked out her tongue and tasted him.

He groaned.

He was sweet and salty. Delicious. She wanted more.

Immensely curious, she bent her head and touched the tip of him with the tip of her tongue. His breathing ratcheted. His cock jumped.

She licked the surface of his head, then swirled her tongue around him. Smiling when he moaned again, she made herself more comfortable between his legs and explored him with her tongue as she had with her fingers. When she couldn't get enough, he pulled the jumpsuit off his torso, raised his hips and slid his pants down, shoving them past his knees to his ankles.

She took a moment to run her hands over his chest and belly, reveling in the feel of muscle contracting under her touch. His chest intrigued her, but now, now she had a greater pleasure waiting for her.

She pushed his knees apart, burrowed in and lapped at his cock. Greedy, hot licks. She traced the pulsing blue vein. She flicked her tongue against the base of his penis, then got as much of him as she could in her mouth. She nibbled, increasing her hunger as well as his. She bit a little harder. When he stilled, going even harder in her mouth, she pulled off him. "You like that?"

"You know I do." His voice was low, hoarse, spoken through tightly drawn lips.

With his eyes looking almost black, barely a distinction between iris and cornea, Adrian looked like a man in deep pain. Or serious pleasure.

"More?" she whispered.

He nodded.

She bent to him again, this time kissing the side of his cock down to the base, licking his balls. He exhaled sharply, and sat very still as she took one in her mouth and rolled it gently. She felt them contract.

"Enough," he ordered.

She pulled back, then felt her back against the carpet as he pushed her down. He stood, kicked off his jumpsuit and soft-soled boots and dropped to his knees beside her. "The first time should be somewhere more comfortable," he apologized, "but you've done your job too well."

He slipped on a condom and came down on top of her. She opened her legs, welcoming him, and drew him closer with an embrace. Her arms stretched around him, palms gliding over his back, feeling the muscles tighten under her touch. She ran one hand up his spine, held his nape, fingers caressing the soft skin and running though his short hair.

His breathing quickened with hers. They lay, forehead to forehead for a moment, gazing intently into the other's eyes. She licked her lips, and then his, as he took her mouth.

It was like the first kiss. Powerful, demanding everything from her. His lips were soft yet insistent. His tongue penetrated her partly opened mouth and explored. In an instant, he changed. The kiss changed.

It was nothing like the first kiss. Possessive, commanding, giving everything to her. She took it, took his tongue, his taste, his mouth and made them hers. This was what she had longed for, craved, to be possessed, to possess.

In moments, they were beyond flashpoint. She lifted her hips in the age-old invitation but he didn't need coaxing. He shoved forward, penetrated her in a sure, forceful thrust that sent fire shooting through her veins.

Sweat beaded his forehead as he set a rhythm, each stroke pushing her higher and higher, stopping her thoughts and forcing her to do no more than feel and accept. He lifted her legs around his waist, grunting with satisfaction when she reached between their bodies and ringed the base of his cock with her fingers.

He didn't need that encouragement. His thrusts became harder and shorter, then slower and deeper, as deep as he could go. His breathing quickened, rasping hot against her neck. She gripped his forearms, his wrists, his thighs, anywhere she could grab, holding on as he propelled her to the top.

Ten, she thought.

Nine. Eight. Sev—*ohmigod,* here it comes!

She came in an exploding gush, clasping him internally and clawing at his thighs. She screamed.

He shouted.

His orgasm followed hers so closely, sparking another from her. She shuddered, convulsing beneath him, barely conscious.

He held her there, suspended while he panted, eyes closed and his chest heaving. Gradually, she became aware of the carpet underneath her butt, the strain on her shoulders, her legs still wrapped around his hips, and the sweat dripping from his chest onto her belly.

After a long moment, he gave his head a shake then opened his eyes and stared down at her. He lowered her legs to the floor and came down beside her, still intimately joined to her body. "All right?"

She couldn't speak, could only look into his dark eyes and nod.

"Did I hurt you?" His solicitude, after causing her deliberate pain during their training sessions, was a tender surprise.

She shook her head. She could feel him, pressed close to her from shoulder to knee, his body hot and damp. His cock rested within her. She reveled in the closeness, in his hard muscles against her softer ones.

"I tried to make it last," she confessed in a drowsy murmur. "I only got to seven."

His low laugh resonated against her chest. "Under the circumstances, that's pretty good."

"It was good, wasn't it?"

His arms tightened around her. "It's not over yet."

She forced her eyes open. "Not?"

His eyes were so close to hers she could drown in their depths. He held her close to him for a moment, a moment in which she forgot to think, to worry, forgot any and everything but the comfort and security she felt in his arms.

He released her long enough to reach for his pants. He dug into a pocket and brought out a chain of beads, varying in size from small at the end to large at the ring handle. They looked like a string of pearls, glistening as he showed them to her.

"These are anal beads," he instructed. "I'm going to put them in you one at a time."

She rolled over and lifted her butt to him. He chuckled and smoothed his palm over her butt cheek. "Very good."

He used the lube on her anus, then carefully inserted the smallest bead. He waited while she accepted that, and then one after the other, he pushed the rest of the beads in. She took them easily, squirming only a little at the largest one. When the last one was in, he patted her butt again. "You please me."

She moaned with pleasure at his words as much as the sensations in her butt as he wiggled the cord and made the beads move in her. At his prompting she moved to her knees and rested her forehead on her hands.

He rose behind her and tugged slightly on the cord. She moaned and waited for more. It wasn't long in coming as he reached under her and caressed the soft bare lips of her pussy.

"So responsive," he murmured. "Always open and ready for me. Does this make you feel good?"

"Mmm, more."

He pinched her clit. "When I say."

"Yes, Adrian," she whispered.

He played with her pussy then moved one hand to her breasts. He cupped one gently, then the other. When her nipples hardened in his hand, he pinched hard, then eased the tiny hurt with soft strokes. Her breathing changed, became fast and hard as her body opened to him. She waited impatiently for him to take her, to plunge his cock into her.

When he did, she inhaled sharply at the swift, deep thrust. She felt him go high into her, filling her completely. She took that first stroke, then all the others as he mounted her without respite. He shoved himself hard into her over and over, as she clamped and clasped him within her. He withdrew enough to create enough space between them to twirl the cord in her ass. She breathed harder, swamped with sensations. He jabbed at her with short strokes as he pulled on the beads.

"When the last one comes out, then you can come."

"Oh yes, yes please," she panted.

She held on, controlling her response as the heat deepened, intensified and her muscles screamed for release. He pulled slowly, and the largest bead popped out. The thrill rushed through her body.

"Not yet!"

He thrust into her again, as if relishing every anguished writhe of her torso. He pulled another bead free, then another and another until only the last one, the smallest one, was still insider her.

"Now, come now," Adrian demanded and pulled the bead loose. As soon as it was free, he plunged into her and pinched one nipple very hard.

She felt no pain. Norris felt only the exquisite release that shattered her senses. Her muscles convulsed around him as she came in a great gush of pleasure. He stiffened behind her, gripped her hip and came himself.

She collapsed under him, her body shaking and exhausted. Adrian came down on top of her, his cock slipping out of her as he rolled to one side. He wrapped his arms around her and pulled her into his torso and groin. They lay there, breathing heavily while their bodies rested.

At last, he withdrew and rose. He disappeared into the bathroom. She heard water running, then he came back to her.

"Up you go."

"I'm tired," she murmured.

"Now, Norris."

His voice, severe and demanding, sank into her. Gone was the tender lover. She forced herself to her knees, then to her feet.

What torment did he have in mind for her now?

Chapter Eleven

He took her hand and led her into the shower. Positioning their bodies under the multiple pulsating jets, he cleansed them both. He had washed her before, many times, his touch impersonal and cool. This time, his hands were hot, his breath blew warm against her skin, and his touch was that of a lover. He let her do nothing, didn't let her touch him as he soaped and washed her in a caress. He turned her in his arms to rinse her, lingered on her breasts and belly, teasing her shaven mound and pussy.

He touched her like he owned her, she thought as he turned her, bent her over and washed her butt, stroking her back before he soaped and washed her anus. The hot water streamed over her, cascading from her spine, easing her muscles, yet she tensed. Quickly, remembering his coaching and his displeasure when she resisted him, she forced herself to relax. She waited, expecting him to enter her, to take her anally, but he merely rimmed her with his finger, awakening the multiple sensitive nerve endings. Her breath quickened. She drew in several, fast, steamy breaths before he urged her upright, holding her back against his chest as he ran his hands over her breasts and down her flanks. How could he arouse her so quickly?

Drowsiness fled, replaced by an increasingly fierce hunger. She stood compliant in his embrace, holding back as he instructed her, while her body craved his.

This was torment indeed.

It astonished her that she could want him with such desperation after the lovemaking they'd just shared. Yet she accepted it as only right and natural that Adrian should command her body to respond to him as he wished.

She lifted her eyes, staring at him over her shoulder. Between the gushing hot water and the steam swirling around and between them, she read approval on his face. Approval and intent. Hungry intent.

He moved her to face the shower enclosure, pressing her breasts against cool glass. He held her, wedged between his chest and the glass while his cock grew between her butt cheeks. She murmured, deep in her throat.

"Good, isn't it?" he whispered against her neck. "Want it to get better?"

Her breathing quickened. He'd been toying with her a few moments ago, letting her guess and anticipate his next move. She knew that this was why he'd prepared her with dildo and butt plug, widening her for a lover's pleasure. She hadn't expected it to be Adrian, but now, how perfect. It had to be Adrian.

She nodded.

"I can't hear you."

"Yes."

His cock circled her anus, withdrew. She moaned and looked over her shoulder to see him reach for a tube of lubricating oil. She waited, expectant and eager, yet shivery with fear. He was big, bigger than any dildo.

Shielding her from the spray, he lubed her ass, working the oil into the tight channel, then smoothed more on himself. He bent her over, widening her stance with his feet, bringing the tip of his penis again to her anus.

She quivered, already anticipating pain.

He pushed in, gently, ever so gently, yet she tensed.

"Easy now." He stroked her upper thigh, reaching higher until he caressed the outer lips of her pussy. "Slow and easy."

She held herself still, forcing herself not to squirm against the pleasure of his finger at her pussy, but to relax, hands pressed against the glass as he pushed in an inch, rested, another inch, rested again.

"Good." He waited, caressing her breasts with one hand, and her clit with the other.

She closed her eyes, surrendering to him, trusting him, pleasure building as heat shot through her from tip to toe. She felt surrounded by him at her back, his arms around her, his cock now working deeper and harder into her.

Aahhh...no dildo ever felt this way! He was hot and hard, a living force within her. She felt her muscles clamp down on him, heard his grunt, and reveled in the way he took her, giving her pleasure even as he took what he wanted from her. He allowed her no respite, fingers busy on her nipples and pussy, cock pushing ever deeper. He pinched one nipple, hard.

She screamed. Pain, pleasure, delight, all mixed together as he broke through the last ring of muscles and claimed her ass for his own.

Stroking now. Out, allowing muscles to tighten. In, forcing them open. Steadily, deeper with each stroke, pushing her against the shower enclosure with each thrust. Her breasts were squashed but she felt no pain, only one hand between them and the glass, working magic with her nipples. He pinched again, harder, then pulled on her nipple until it grew as hard as his cock working its magic within her.

Heat. Steam. Noise.

Her breathing and his harsh above the pounding water. Her face pushed against the glass, peering through it. In the mirror beyond, shapes misted by steam, coming together in age-old mating.

Such coming together! She couldn't bear it, couldn't take another moment. He paused, gathering himself, then shoved forward. Blistering. Steam. Filled to her depths, she convulsed, shattering in his arms.

Only his cock and his embrace kept her from collapsing. He held her tightly, pumped once, twice, three times and came himself. She felt him shoot high into her, his gush a liquid heat even hotter than his cock rammed into her as far as it would go. She shuddered, accepting his possession.

They sank to their knees as he pulled out of her. Hot water rained down on them, cleansing, and steam rose up high about them, cocooning them in their own world of sensation and satiation.

At last, long moments later, he roused. He reached for the scented bath gel and cleansed her inside and out. She was still, receiving everything he did to her, for her.

She felt fulfilled, every fantasy come true. Cosseted, loved and womanly. Adrian rested himself, back propped against the wall, eyes closed. She studied him through the spray, seeing his face relaxed and at ease.

If she'd ever thought he was severe, unfeeling, and coldhearted, she had only to see him like this and know how much control he exerted over himself. He was a different person. Not a trainer demanding obedience, but a lover commanding her body, coaxing from her desires and sensations she'd never thought to experience.

She didn't know how long they stayed there, heaped together on the shower floor. At last, though, they roused and turned off the water. They dried each other with warmed towels, and stumbled toward her bed, where they fell into a deep sleep with their arms clasped around each other.

Hours later, she woke, to find herself on her back, Adrian already in her deep and hard. She opened her mouth to speak, but he shushed her with his lips and tongue. She sucked him in, his tongue filling her mouth as his cock did her pussy.

She didn't know how long he'd been in her, knew only that he was hard, his breath coming fast. She reached between them, clasping his cock at the base, cupping his balls, already hard and high in their sac. She murmured her pleasure.

He bucked against her hand and increased his pace, taking her with him. She was hot and liquid around him, could feel his strokes deep within her, feel his weight heavy against her.

"More," she panted, already catching up with him, fevered and reaching for release.

"Like this?" He thrust deep, losing control and spasming convulsively as she felt her orgasm lift her and propel her out of mind.

She called his name. He grunted hers. They locked together, straining as their mutual orgasm went on and on. Their bodies shook, convulsed in delight. She felt every little quiver, every major tremor as he plunged deep, deeper still and finally convulsed. He collapsed, heavy on her, his breath harsh against her temple.

He started to roll away, but she brought her arms up close around him and clutched him within her legs. "Not yet."

She couldn't bear to let him go, couldn't bear to lose the closeness, the intimacy of the moment. She held him tightly, holding on, until nature took over and sleep eased her grip.

When she woke, she roused enough to prop herself up on an elbow. She studied his body, lax in sleep, yet his muscles were clearly defined in shoulders, chest, abdomen and thighs. One hand lay curled over his chest, the fingers loosely curved. She studied his fingernails, short, clean and trimmed, and remembered how skillfully he'd used his fingers and hands to arouse her, penetrate her and increase her pleasure. She all but shuddered with the memory of him buried so deep in her that she couldn't believe he wasn't created to be an integral part of her.

His belly was flat and hard. She was tempted to stroke, to explore but didn't want to wake him. She leaned closer to his face, examining every feature. His eyes were closed, a smile softening the severe contours of his face. She'd pleased him.

And pleased herself. As hard, as heart-stopping and as often as he'd made her come, it wasn't until they came in that mind-blowing simultaneous orgasm that she knew what all the fuss was about. It could actually happen. And it had!

Ah sex, glorious sex. No, that wasn't right. It was as Adrian had stressed. This was making love, intimacy, not mechanics or purely physical sensation, and it was more than glorious. It surpassed definition, that closeness, the oneness of two bodies meshed together, shattering together.

It felt like being in love.

Love? Where had that idea come from? She explored it gingerly, testing it carefully. It was too easy, predictable even, to let her emotions be overcome by physical sensation. When she was weak and spineless like this, she was too susceptible. Too ready to believe that there could be anything more between them than extraordinarily good sex.

No, it wasn't love. Couldn't be.

She sighed.

He opened one eye and winked at her.

Winked! The austere, stern robotron had loosened up enough to wink at her. She giggled.

"What amuses you?" he asked through a yawn.

"You. You're completely different."

"You only saw one side of me before this." He indicated the rumpled bed, the sheets half off the mattress and the pillows on the floor.

"The tidy side." She smirked.

"Complaining?"

She lowered her head and licked his collarbone, delighting in his instantaneous shiver. Where was his vaunted control now?

Abruptly, she raised her head. "Why were you so mean to me?"

He raised an eyebrow. "Define mean."

"You know, mean. Tying me to that bar, leaving me alone, hanging like a side of beef." She scowled at both the humiliating, painful memories and his apparent lack of concern.

"Do I have to explain my methods?"

She nodded.

He pulled her closer, nuzzled her breasts. "Now?"

Norris pulled away. "Now. I want you to tell me why you were beastly and Rachel got the same results with praise and respect."

He exhaled, then reached for a pillow and settled it behind his back. He looked at her with an expression she couldn't quite decipher. Doubt, maybe? "Do you think Rachel would have gotten those same results from you when you first started here?" His eyes narrowed. "Be honest."

She considered that. She'd come in eager to leave svelte and sexy, thinking she was ready to do whatever it took to reach her goal, but truthfully? Given her past history with diets and nutrition, she'd have followed her usual path and quit fairly soon. She would have tried the exercise routines, gotten bored and quit. She'd have railed against the spartan fare, delicious as it was, and quit.

"You'd have quit on her, right?"

She scowled at him.

"Right. So I made it hard for you. Demanded more of you. Made you hate me enough to want to show me. Prove me wrong about you." He looked deep into her eyes. "It worked, didn't it?"

"You didn't have to like it so damn much," she muttered.

"Like it?" He groaned. "You have no idea how hard it was."

"Yeah?" She felt a smile begin, then grow. "Harder than with other clients?"

"I don't discuss my clients," he stated flatly.

"Well," she studied him speculatively, "I can say this much. You must have played the ogre often enough to get it down pat."

He chuckled. "Ogre. Beast. Thanks a lot."

"I don't like to think of you having sex with other clients," she admitted. "Other women," she added, voicing her deepest anguish.

He pulled her into his arms. "What's done is done."

She held back, then gave in and nestled close to his chest. He stroked her back, and cradled her head in his palm. At last, she murmured, "It's just that when I leave here, I hate to think of you doing the same thing to other women that you did with me."

He blew out his breath. "I'm not going to discuss this with you."

She blinked hard, then rolled off the bed. Heading for the shower, she looked back. He had moved to the edge of the bed, sitting with his feet on the floor, elbows on his knees, hands clasped between his legs, head lowered. He looked like a man in pain, at the least, in confusion.

Join the club.

When she came out of the shower, after having briskly applied the loofah and then the assorted creams and lotions Rachel had given her, Adrian was gone. He'd tidied up the bed, leaving no trace of his being there.

She checked the living room and the training room. Both were empty. If she still wasn't sore and her breasts full, she'd have imagined his ever being there. Ever making love.

Damn him.

The door to her suite opened quietly. She whirled, expecting to see Adrian, but it was only a member of the staff delivering her breakfast. She set the table, placed several dishes on it and left, as wordless as ever.

Norris poured herself a glass of juice. Hungrily, she sat and began to eat. She'd taken the last bite of her omelet *aux fines herbes* when Rachel entered.

"Good. Ready for your weigh-in?"

Norris nodded, but felt strangely reluctant. She could tell by her body, toned and fit now after weeks of exercise and proper nutrition, that she had lost more weight. She felt good, energetic and healthy.

She also felt sad, but that wasn't part of the regimen. That was her own personal contribution. Still, she rose and joined Rachel.

After she'd weighed in and been measured as she had been the first day, Angela hugged her. "Congratulations! You've lost thirty-four pounds!"

Norris' eyes widened. "I did it? Really did it?"

"You really did. See?" Angela showed her the chart, with her beginning weight and measurements. Then pointed at the last entry. She'd really done it. She'd reached her goal.

She felt proud. Satisfied, eager to share the good news, but at the same time, felt uneasy. She'd come this far. What would happen next?

Angela answered the question. "You still have a few days left with us. You'll see the nutritionist again, use any of our guest services, and if you like, consult our personal shopper." Angela grinned at the look on her face. "You want to leave in the same clothes you wore coming in?"

"I hadn't thought of that. No way!"

"Let's make an appointment for you, then."

The next few days were busy. Rachel instructed her on a workout routine she could do at home and one for the gym. The nutritionist put together a customized eating regimen based on her likes and dislikes. She had her nails done, a complete wax and facial, her hair styled and felt buffed, shined and polished, ready to face the world.

But not naked.

After hours with the personal shopper, who took her measurements, discussed her lifestyle and made some suggestions, Norris began trying on the clothes the shopper brought back on approval.

Some she discarded immediately. Some she bought, anticipating the looks she'd get when she returned to work wearing her closely fitted new suits. Some she adored, including the new sexy lingerie and the casual clothes that showed off her new figure. With the exception of the outfit she'd wear to leave, everything else was delivered to her apartment.

Her days were full getting ready to pick up the threads of her old life. Still she had time to worry about Adrian, how he risked his job to be with her. She knew he violated policy by becoming personally involved with her. She felt ashamed she almost wished he'd get fired. She didn't really want that, she realized, but if he no longer worked at *Sweet Discipline*, would they continue to see each other? Could they have more nights like the ones they shared here, exploring and discovering new worlds with him? He dominated her senses as he did her body. If she'd thought they couldn't surpass their first simultaneous orgasm, he proved her wrong.

He used her body, and his, relentlessly. When she complained she couldn't take any more, he showed her she could. He used the bedroom toys, more than once inserting the Ben Wa balls and licking her clit while she thrashed about and begged him to remove the balls and let her come.

Always, always, he pushed her to the edge, kept her hanging, made her wait, demanding she control her body, until at last, he allowed her release. She did everything he demanded of her. Any position, any time, any part of her body.

He taught her the wicked, overwhelming pleasures of dildo and cock thrusting into her pussy and anus. When the dildos and anal beads weren't enough, he used her body as he pleased, and in pleasing himself he showered pleasure almost beyond endurance upon her. He gave her no rest. She took all he gave her and craved more.

More of Adrian, of all he was as man and lover. The more she knew of him in that way, the more she realized how little she knew of him as a person. One night, as they lay closely entwined, muscles relaxing, she said as much.

"What do you want to know?" he asked, his voice slow and deep.

"What do you do for fun, when you're not working?"

"I exercise. Play some ball, go out with friends."

It sounded so normal, so everyday. "What else? Where do you go for vacations?"

He stretched, then pulled her close again. "Places I haven't been before."

"Where did you go last?"

"Trekking in Tibet." He yawned. "Before that, I hiked in Torres del Paine. That's in southern Chile. Cold, windy but beautiful."

Ugh. "Don't you ever take cruises, soak up the rays?"

"Boring."

She liked nothing better. "Well, what do you watch on TV?"

"Not much. Some sports, History channel, the news."

Didn't this man do anything she liked to do? "How about food? What's your favorite meal?"

"I'm a vegetarian. Veggies. Salads, fruits."

Oh no. She loved thick steaks, pork chops and hamburgers. She sighed. "Well, where do you live?"

"I have an apartment in the building."

She rolled over to look at him. "You live here?"

"It's convenient."

And not accessible.

"I also have a place at the beach."

She perked up. "That must be nice. Sand, surf, sunbathing."

"Bad for your skin." He smoothed his hand over her shoulder, cupped her breast and squeezed gently. "I like yours like this. Soft, white, like silk."

Her nipple peaked immediately. He pinched it, softly at first, then harder, giving her pain he followed quickly with pleasure when he sucked her nipple into his mouth and caressed it with his tongue. She responded as she always did, quickly and completely.

His mouth left her breast. He tongued his way down her belly, pausing to explore her navel, then unerringly found her pussy. Though she was still sated, her body opened to him without demur. He licked and nibbled, pausing only to praise her nude pussy lips. She squirmed with the heat growing in her, then complained when he lifted his head.

"On your knees."

She rolled and lifted herself into position, head resting on her crossed wrists, butt elevated, knees spread wide. He stroked her spine, then cupped her butt cheeks, pushing them together, then separating them for his tongue. He licked her from spine to rosebud, then rimmed her, bringing each nerve ending to life. She waited, expectantly, impatiently, her breath coming harder and faster. How would he take her?

One hand delved between her legs, seeking entrance. One finger circled her pussy, then slid in. She needed more, and he responded with another finger, then two, then four held closely together. She clenched around him.

"More?" he whispered.

"Yes, yes," she whimpered. "More!"

He pulled back his hand, ignoring her complaints, and moved to lie at her side. "Stay," he instructed when she started to drop to the bed. She did as he said, lifting one leg for him to slide under her. She thought he wanted her to ride him, something he seldom did, but which she enjoyed tremendously. Instead, he slid until his head was under her pussy. She lowered herself to him. He licked her, his tongue caressing her clit and pushing into her pussy. She moaned with the pleasure, but it was cut short when he pulled away. In moments, though, his fingers replaced his tongue.

She realized he had his fingers in her up to his knuckles, pushing in and out, each time deeper, until his hand was almost completely inside her. Fascinated, she watched hardly believing that she could take so much of him and not feel pain. She felt the knobs of his knuckles against the thin walls of her pussy, caressing her, stroking her internally. She moaned again. It was so good, and still, she wanted more.

As if he understood, he pulled his hand out. She looked down, between her legs and saw him tuck his thumb into his palm. She held her breath. He couldn't! He wouldn't be able to get his entire hand in her. He inserted his fingers again, pushing gently but inexorably deeper into her.

She gasped as she watched his hand disappear. Her juices flowed, easing his way, yet she held herself stiffly. He flicked her a glance, read the uncertainty on her face. "I'm fisting you, Norris."

"I can't. You can't…"

"I am and you will."

She obeyed him in this as in everything else. She widened herself, taking him in inch by inch, feeling her inner muscles expand to accept his fingers, his knuckles, then his palm, and with a last push, he was in her up to his wrist. She gasped, then moaned with delight as his fingers brushed the entrance to her womb. Such a caress! So deep, so intimate, so overwhelming. In that moment, his hand holding her entire femininity, she surrendered herself completely. He held her, in his hand, while he told her what he felt, what he owned. "This is mine, Norris."

She said nothing, could say nothing. She closed her eyes and gave herself up to the pleasure. He caressed her intimately again, then slowly withdrew his hand. She clenched, her pussy missing him. She waited, longing to be filled again, while he changed position and came up on his knees behind her. He teased her with his cock while her reached under her and used her juices to lubricate her anus. She waited, holding her breath, while he pushed himself into her.

He grunted with the effort when her ass muscles resisted, then exhaled when they surrendered to his possession. He pushed in until his cock was buried to the hilt, then with a satisfied murmur, claimed her ass for himself. He pushed in, withdrew, and pushed in repeatedly while she quivered and shook under his assault. He reached between her legs and pulled at her clit, then shoved his fingers into her pussy. Doubly impaled, she cried out.

"Please, now, Adrian!"

"When I tell you," he snapped.

She bore his thrusts, her breath hot against her wrists, her breasts full and hungry. She grabbed one and mimicked Adrian's tweaks, pulling and pinching her nipple as he continued to thrust into her ass. At last, when she though she could bear it no longer, her ass on fire and her pussy drenched, he shouted, "Now!"

She obeyed instantly. Her muscles clamped around his fingers. Her ass clenched his cock as he gave a mighty thrust of his hips and embedded himself in her. She felt him shaking and convulsing in her, behind her, and collapsed on the bed. He followed her down, still in her, still shaking with the combined forces of their orgasms.

Hours later, when she roused, sore in both her ass and her pussy, Adrian tended to her. He lifted her from the bed and carried her into the bath, where he ran a tub and lowered them both into the steaming water. They were silent, content to bask in the heat and in each other. As the water cooled, they bathed each other, gently washing his cock and balls, her pussy and ass. They left the tub, dried and fell into bed again. Norris was sure she'd never experience anything as sweet and peaceful as this again.

In the morning, waking by herself, Norris reached for Adrian and found his side of the bed cold and empty. She felt lonely even as she told herself that Adrian had to leave her before anyone saw him. She reassured herself it was for his benefit, that he shouldn't risk his job, but it was hard not to want to be with him all the time. She tried to balance the way she felt when Adrian took possession of her body with the encroaching end of her stay at *Sweet Discipline*. She hated each passing minute, knowing how they limited her time with Adrian.

She'd been crazy to even think she might be in love with him. They had nothing in common. Nothing but the insatiable sexual need for each other.

With each lovemaking session, her control grew. On the occasion she reached the count of two, he prolonged her orgasm so long and so thoroughly that she lapsed into unconsciousness, the *petit morte*, and roused only when he took her into the tub and washed her from head to toe. He'd cradled her, kissing her temples, her cheek, the side of her neck, propping her with his arms under hers. She had to work hard to keep tears from revealing her emotional response to his tender care.

She didn't want to end their affair. She wanted Adrian to be a part of her new life and imagined ways they could manage it. But he said nothing. No matter how thoroughly he loved her, how he dominated her body and her senses, or how sated he left her, he made no mention of the time after she'd gone. The hours left to her with him took on a new intensity, a desperate feeling of hanging on to moments vanishing much too quickly.

One night, she dared say as much. He had just unwrapped her legs from his waist, rolled off her body, and gathered her close. With her face nestled between his chest and neck, her body sated and boneless, she heard the words before she could hold them back.

He pulled away from her. "You don't know what you're asking for."

She looked into his face. In the dimness of her bedroom, his eyes were dark and fathomless. She sensed his disapproval, his retreat, and grabbed his shoulders. "Is it so wrong to want to hold on to what we have?"

He blew out a noisy breath. "You'll forget me when you leave here."

"I won't. How can you make light of this? Of us?"

"I don't make light of anything, Norris. You've got what you came for. We're both satisfied."

"Maybe I'm not," she retorted. "Maybe I want more."

"Be still, Norris."

"No, not this time." Realizing the risk she took in disobeying him, she took a deep breath and sat up to face him. "You've made love to me. You claimed my pussy. You said it was yours! And now you're going to let me leave and that's it?"

In an instant, he kicked back the covers and rose to his knees. Before she could protest, he rolled her over on her belly and lifted her to her knees. She whimpered when he spread her butt cheeks apart and reached for the tube of lube. Tears formed as he lubricated her anus and the largest of the dildos. She sobbed as he inserted it, slowly and inescapably. This smacked of discipline, of punishment, making her remember how it felt to be restrained on the workout table while he trained her muscles to accept and control her responses. She crawled forward, but he pulled her back. She tried again, and he slapped her butt.

She cried out. "No, Adrian. Not like this!"

"Be still," he repeated, his voice cold and stern.

She inhaled deeply, through her tears, relaxing her inner muscles, relinquishing her body to him. He was efficient, arousing her with dildo and his fingers in her pussy until she cried, resisting his order to come.

"Please, Adrian, not like this. Come in me, please, oh, please," she gasped when he pushed the dildo in farther than it had ever been before. She screamed, stretched wider, pushed harder, taking it deeper, more painfully. More pleasurably.

"Please, Adrian."

He slapped her butt again, once on each cheek. It hurt, but she clamped her lips shut and took the discipline. Abruptly, he pulled out the dildo, and thrust his cock into her instead. The pulsating satin heat of him, after insensate rubber and latex, convulsed her. Her muscles spasmed, provoking him into his own passion.

He pulled her hard onto him, giving her no choice but to take, to move with him, to slide off, be yanked back, as he pushed her higher, harder and longer. At last, tears falling freely, she could take no more, barely hanging on while he pumped again and again.

"Now," he grunted. "Now. Come. Give it to me."

At his command, she let go, unleashing the orgasm he demanded. She came and came, muscles shattering and convulsing around his still thrusting cock.

He groaned, and shot hard into her. His grip loosened on her hips and she collapsed face down on the rumpled sheets. He followed her down, pressing her deeper into the mattress as he used her body as a pillow, his cock still embedded in her ass. His breath rasped into her ear, his breath seared her neck.

She couldn't breathe. She found the strength to twitch. He rolled off her, falling on his back beside her. When she was able, she propelled herself out of bed and into the shower. She expected him to join her, as he'd done countless times before, but he didn't. When she went back into the bedroom, he was gone.

All that remained was the heady aroma of sex.

She was given the chance to leave a day early and rejected it. She wanted the last night with Adrian, to make it right with him, and ached for his touch when she slept in an empty bed.

She expected Adrian at any moment her last day, dreaded saying goodbye to him. She didn't want it to end here, like this. She wanted to see him again to ask why he'd demeaned their last encounter, made it mechanical, made it sex, when they should have been making love. She didn't want to leave without making love to him again. At the same time, she had to see him to put away her feelings about him, to put closure to them.

But he didn't come. She sent a message to him, but he didn't respond. She waited, hour after hour, pretending she didn't see the pointed looks of staff who came to her door.

At last, though, she had no excuse, no reason to prolong her stay. The exit interview with the director was surprisingly difficult.

Wearing yet another severely cut black dress, the director sat behind her minimalist desk and looked at her coldly. "Everything has been satisfactory? You've met your goals. The staff has provided you with all the material you need?"

"Yes."

She glanced at her file, then frowned. "I see you changed trainers. Most unusual." She focused a glare on Norris.

"It wasn't my choice. I mean, not after the first day," Norris explained. "About Adrian—"

The director's glare became more pronounced. "You have a complaint about him?"

"Ah, no, that is, I'd like to see him before I leave."

The director closed the file with a snap. "That won't be possible."

"I wanted to ah..."

"Leave him a gratuity? I see you left one for other staff. Shall we add one for him? On your charge?"

A tip for Adrian? She'd never even thought of it, but she supposed it must be customary. But a tip? For services rendered above and beyond? She hadn't minded leaving a very generous tip for the steward on the cruise liner, but that was different. She'd felt nothing for him. She knew as soon as she was off the ship and it sailed again, there'd be other women, as lonely and needy as herself.

She could say the same thing about her time at *Sweet Discipline*, but tipping Adrian was different. Leaving him money changed the situation. It lessened the connection between them and made the time she'd spent with him somehow dirty. Shameful. Still, when the director continued to look at her with a questioning expression, she nodded.

She walked out of *Sweet Discipline* without a second glance.

Chapter Twelve

"Norris, you look fantastic!"

Her staff clustered around her office door, looking her over with astounded eyes. She turned, showing off both her slim figure and her new designer suit, laughing at the more outrageous compliments and fielding questions about where she'd been and how she'd gotten such a great new look.

At last, she eyed the neat stacks of paper on her desk, and made shooing gestures. "Scram, all of you. I've got a ton of catching up to do."

She was focused on a report when a knock at the door caught her attention. She glanced up. "Hi, Jack."

"I heard the talk," he began with an admiring, thorough scan, "so I had to see for myself. Whatever you did made a new woman out of you."

He'd noticed! He'd come himself to check her out. Even as her pulse jumped, she kept her voice cool. "Thanks."

"Stand up. Let's have a look at you."

She felt something slither down her back. Those were Adrian's words, and he wasn't Adrian. Still, Adrian had shown her he had no more interest in her. She remembered her fantasies about Jack that had taken her to *Sweet Discipline* and, forcing a smile, did as Jack asked. Even turned around so he could get a good look, quelling the unease in her belly. Somehow, though Adrian had said nothing about an ongoing relationship, she still felt committed to him. Felt like she betrayed him by showing off for another man.

"Who would have believed it? You're beautiful."

Weeks before, she'd have basked in his attention. It felt good, to be praised and flattered, but somehow coming from Jack Rodriguez, it sound it sounded over the top, smarmy. Empty.

Where he'd never before done more than pause in her doorway, acting as if he had more important places to be, people to see, now he sat in her office chair, propped one ankle over a knee and looked like he was there for the duration.

Once she'd have jumped for joy, now she settled herself behind her desk. "I've got a lot of work here."

He spared a glance for her desk. "So I see." He turned his smile on full voltage. "Let's catch up tonight over a drink. Dinner, too?"

Six weeks ago, those words would have been heaven. The way he was ogling her, his gaze lingering at the vee of her jacket as if he was sizing up her measurements, made her distinctly uncomfortable. She'd yearned to be sleek and sexy to catch his eye and get him into bed, but looking at him now, it wouldn't be much of a challenge. One she didn't want to test.

The realization left her disoriented and unbalanced. She couldn't fault the results, but her reasons for going to *Sweet Discipline* had been off. Way off.

She had the distinct notion that all it would take would be to lean over the desk, give him a good eyeful and whisper, "Take me," and he'd be out of that chair with his pants around his knees in record time.

She flipped open her laptop. "Ask me later," she said, though she knew if he came back, she'd be waving him off. So much for her fantasy of throwing him to the ground and having her way with him until he cried uncle.

Damn Adrian. How could he do this to her?

As soon as she was alone, she closed her office door, picked up the phone and dialed Kendra. When she heard her friend's voice, she said, "You owe me lunch."

"You're back! You did it, the whole six weeks?"

"I did. Wait until you see me."

"I can't wait!" Kenny sounded excited and curious. "Can you do dinner tonight, instead of lunch? I know it's short notice, but I'm dying to see the results."

Norris thought briefly of Jack's invitation. "Sure."

They named the time and place, and when Norris arrived, running a few minutes late, Kendra was already seated with a glass of wine. She stood when she spotted Norris.

They hugged, then Kendra stood back to inspect Norris who was wearing one of her new, petite and skimpy dresses. "God, you look wonderful! What did you lose? Twenty pounds?"

Norris smiled. "Thirty-four."

Kendra's eyes widened. "Amazing," she breathed. "You did it. You stuck it out and now look at you. I am impressed. So proud of you!"

Norris basked in her friend's praise. They chatted of this and that until they'd ordered.

"Okay, now we can talk," Kendra prompted.

"Good." There was a lot she wanted to know, beginning with how Adrian had known so much about her. "What did you tell them about me?"

Kendra looked taken aback at her accusing tone. "When I recommended you, I had to fill out an information form."

"And..."

"And they wanted to know about your personality, your personal traits—"

"And you told them I was obstinate and didn't play well with others?"

Kendra blinked. "No. I told them you were a successful consultant. In demand. I said you are persistent and committed to your work."

Then how did Adrian know so she was obstinate and stubborn? She could almost hear his cold voice telling her she was willful and temperamental. Where would he have gotten that if Kendra hadn't told him? And what about the other things he knew about her? "You told them about getting dumped and being depressed?"

"Well," Kendra dragged the syllable out, "I did mention you'd gained weight and couldn't seem to get it off after that happened."

So. Some of the intimate information about her had come from Kendra. That meant Adrian knew the rest about her because they'd dug into her personal life. How? Who had they talked to?

"Relax. They research everyone. Didn't they have a custom program for you?"

"You bet they did." Norris didn't try to hide her sarcasm.

"Evidently it worked."

Norris wasn't appeased. "Who was your trainer?"

"Adrian. What a hunk." Kendra sighed. "And you?"

"Same here." Norris leaned forward. "Did he do any funny stuff?"

Kendra's brow wrinkled. "Funny how?"

"Ropes, sexual—"

"You're kidding!" Kendra broke in. "Adrian did that? I don't believe it. All he did was work me to death."

Norris sank back against her chair. "No bedroom toys? No offers to teach you better sexual techniques?"

Kendra's mouth dropped. She snapped it shut. She took a sip of wine. "You're telling me that Adrian abused you sexually?"

Abuse? Didn't that imply a lack of consent? Maltreatment? Norris toyed with the napkin on her lap as she remembered being tethered, secured to the workout table and forced to submit, to take whatever discipline Adrian handed out. Pain and humiliation had been a constant thing until she learned to work with Adrian instead of against him. Was that abuse? Or was there a fine line between teaching her control and controlling her? She didn't know. She didn't even care. It was over, done with, and she had the results she wanted.

Kendra took her silence for agreement. "You should report him! That's wrong."

"I signed the contract, and when he asked, I agreed."

"Did you know what he was asking?" Kenny demanded, her voice sharp.

"Not really. Not at first. But later, I agreed."

"That was dumb."

Yes, it was, and she'd suffered for it, but once she'd submitted and handed control of her body to Adrian, how simple it was. And, oh, how she'd exulted in her nights with him.

"What exactly did he do?" Kendra leaned over the table, curiosity rampant.

Norris hesitated. Even if *Sweet Discipline's* contract demanded confidentiality, she didn't want to reveal the mortification she'd endured. Or how, gradually, Adrian had broken her will and her obstinate temper and rebuilt her into a woman more pleasing to him.

Then why didn't he want to keep her? After going to the effort of breaking her down and forcing her to surrender to him, why did he let her leave as if she meant nothing to him? Those were the questions that stuck in her mind, like rubbing salt into open wounds.

Why did he treat her like that? Why her? Why was her program so different than Kendra's? Why was he so angry with her that he wouldn't see her before she left? Or had he chalked her up to one client contract fulfilled and another was on the way? Those thoughts rankled. She'd thought they shared something special, the way he'd claimed her body as his, treated her with gentleness and compassion when she hurt. After he'd hurt her! But the hurt was forgotten in the overwhelming passion he'd shown her. She couldn't forget those nights...

"Norris?"

Kendra's question claimed her attention. So many unanswered questions and one only she could answer. Was she herself pleased with the new Norris?

She flicked a glance down at herself. Her breasts lifted proudly in her new nothing there bra. Her belly was flat, her thighs and hips thinner. Her arm, resting on the table, was slender, more muscular, stronger.

Her willpower held firm. She'd ordered broiled fish and vegetables, without even looking at the heavily sauced or pasta dishes. She could congratulate herself on that much.

Yes, she was pleased with herself. She'd lost the weight, gotten skinny and sexy. She had no complaints on that score.

"Well?" Kendra prompted. "What did he do?"

Norris took a sip of her iced water. She had no wish to reveal the private moments, good or bad, with Adrian. "Client confidentiality, remember?"

Kendra scowled. "You can't hint at what happened and then leave me hanging."

Norris ignored that as she tried to ignore the memories of Adrian with her, flesh on flesh, buried so deep within her, she'd never forget the feel of him.

Yet, try as she might, she couldn't forget something else. "I wonder how many other women Adrian's treated the same way," Norris murmured. "And why me?"

"Because you're gullible. Dumb. Much as I love you, Norris, you're an idiot."

Kenny's words stung. Okay, so she didn't have all the experience that her very married friend had, but she was smart, intelligent and determined. She wasn't some patsy for Adrian to torment and use for his own pleasure.

And hers. She couldn't forget that.

Oh, God, no, she couldn't forget the brain-stopping, out-of-body sheer physical pleasure.

But why her?

Chapter Thirteen

The next morning, Norris called *Sweet Discipline* and asked to speak with Adrian. The receptionist gave her his voicemail.

"Why me, Adrian?" she asked. "What makes me different from other clients? How could you treat me that way?" She hesitated, then asked the questions that kept her awake nights. "Or was I no different? Do you do the same to other women?" She left her phone numbers and waited for an answer.

For three weeks, she followed her new eating plan, exercised regularly, worked out, and exulted in the new contracts she negotiated. For three weeks, while her business profited, she waited for Adrian to call.

For three weeks, she put Jack off. He spent more time in her office, wanting to personally discuss something that could have been handled in a quick email. He made a point of seeing her at least daily, and every time, he asked the same question.

"When are you going to give me the time of day, Norris?"

Good question. Two months ago she'd have jumped at the first invitation, hardly daring to believe he'd asked. She'd have indulged in all her fantasies of stripping him naked and having her way with him.

"How about dinner? Someplace quiet where we can get to know each other?"

She glanced up from her laptop. How well did she want to get to know him? He was dressed in Armani, the beautifully cut jacket resting easily on his broad shoulders and hinting at a tapered waist. He was clean-shaven, hair styled well, his dark looks attractive and oh so sexy.

Why wasn't she turned on? Maybe if she saw him alone, after-hours, the feeling would return. She propped her chin on her fist. "Okay."

His smile oozed sex. "You mean it? Great. I know just the place."

They arranged to meet, though he resisted. "Hey, my mama told me it was important to escort a lady."

What his mama hadn't stressed hard enough was that by allowing him to escort a lady home, the lady might be setting herself up for a one-on-one she didn't particularly want.

"I'll meet you there," she said firmly.

When she walked into the restaurant later, wearing something by a hot new designer, it was worth it to see his eyes pop. Every ache, every drop of sweat, every humiliation she'd endured at *Sweet Discipline* was worth this reaction.

She was slim, svelte and sexy.

Oh, yeah. That felt good. Knowing other men watched her as they made their way to the table added to her pleasure, yet having Jack eye her like he wanted to gobble her up made her uncomfortable. He flirted, he made innuendoes, he talked about work just long enough to emphasize their connection. He talked about himself. He even seemed interested in her experiences and beliefs.

It meant nothing.

She'd given him a chance by accepting his invitation, cautioning herself to keep an open mind, but by the time their dessert was served, she'd made up her mind.

He might be attracted to her. In fact, he made no effort to hide his intent to get her in the sack. It should have been her fantasies coming to life.

Pity she had no intention of letting Jack get anywhere near her toned body.

She went through the motions, though, as they shared a dessert and enjoyed a leisurely after-dinner coffee. She kept her eyes on him as he talked, laughed at his jokes, allowed the eye contact to linger.

She even allowed him to put his hand on her shoulder, fingers casually brushing her breast, when he helped her with her coat. He called her a cab, and holding the door open for her, he leaned in for a kiss.

Testing herself, she allowed that, too. Before *Sweet Discipline*, before Adrian, she'd have melted in a puddle right there on the street when his lips touched hers, and his tongue insinuated its way into her mouth.

It lasted only a moment. She pulled back and slid into the cab. "See you."

The look on his face sparked her guilt complex. She'd led him on, then backed off. Not a nice thing to do, but all in the name of checking herself out, it worked for her.

She wasn't attracted to him.

He was one of the main reasons for her getting thin and sexy and now she couldn't stand the thought of him touching her ever again. She choked back a bitter laugh. She'd put herself through weeks of agony so she could jump Jack's bones and now the idea disgusted her. She'd suffered humiliation and pain from Adrian, then experienced a pleasure with him she was never going to know again, and all for what?

She got out of the cab at her apartment building, noting the admiring glance at her long legs from a passing male, and smiled at the doorman holding the door for her. Her emotional life was in turmoil, but physically, she was in better shape than ever before. She straightened her spine as she entered the elevator. No matter what else happened, she was never going to let herself go again.

And what's more, she'd forget Adrian, too.

She carried that conviction through her door, into the shower and back into her living room in a new short silk robe. She had just poured herself a glass of wine when the doorbell rang. Jack? Had he followed her home?

She checked the security locks. They were all safely secured. She peered through the peephole and recoiled.

"Let me in, Norris."

That voice, severe and commanding as ever! Heart racing, she turned and pressed her back against the door, as if holding shut a door already closed and locked could keep Adrian out. "Why?"

"You asked me a question. Don't you want an answer?"

She turned and peeked at him again. "It doesn't matter anymore."

"Liar. If it was important to you to ask, you want to know."

"Okay, so what is it?"

"Not like this." He gestured with his head at the empty hallway.

Even through the thick wooden door, she felt his presence. Looking into his face, distorted as it was by the peephole, tugged at something within her. The habit of submission to him was still strong, overriding caution. With a muttered curse, she unlocked the door.

He came in, wearing his customary black in a suit, shirt and tie, looking stark, menacing and angry. She flicked a glance at his eyes, noted their depths and without thinking, sank to her knees.

He stood over her, the tips of his polished shoes an inch from her kneecaps. Her palms rested open on her thighs.

"I see you haven't forgotten. That's good."

She kept her head down, eyes intent on his black loafers. Pleasure at his praise trickled through her, weakening her resolve against him.

"Stand."

She got to her feet, gracefully now after weeks of his training, and stood before him, as if still waiting for instructions.

He advanced into her living room, studying her books, her long, low couch and the two upholstered chairs on either side of a gas fireplace. "Very nice." He turned back to her. "May I sit?"

She blinked. She wasn't used to him asking her permission for anything. She gestured to the couch, then perched on the edge of a chair.

"Why you, Norris? What makes you different from other clients?" he prompted.

"You tell me."

He settled back, making himself comfortable against the soft, plush cushions. "Are most of my clients their own worst enemies? No. Are most of my clients stubborn, intractable and lazy? Not all. Are most of my clients a fascinating mix of innocence and earth mother allure? Hardly."

She narrowed her eyes at him. There was a compliment in there somewhere, but she resented his description of her as stubborn and lazy.

Well, lazy.

"Only one is all that."

"Me, I suppose," she said in a pique.

He nodded. "I decided to be your trainer when I read your profile. I needed a challenge. I was getting bored with the usual client, eager and willing—"

"To have sex with you?" she burst in.

He shook his head in admonishment. "To get the most from the program. To make every moment count."

"That's what I wanted."

"That what you thought you wanted," he corrected her flatly. "But what you thought you wanted and what you were prepared to do were two different things."

"And you knew all that from my profile?" she asked, her voice scornful and doubting.

"Partly. I'd also seen you."

"So you decided I wasn't good enough for the usual program and you made one up for me out of Marquis de Sade's handy-dandy spa suggestions?"

He laughed, his amusement filling the room. "It worked, didn't it?"

She jumped to her feet. "If you came here just to laugh at me—"

He rose, too. "No. I came to see how you're doing. Take off that robe and show me."

She clutched the lapels closer over her breasts. The silk rasped against her nipples, a soft, seductive reminder that Adrian liked to brush his palms over them, pull and tweak them until they peaked. "I'm not at *Sweet Discipline* anymore. I don't have to do a thing you say."

"No?" He came closer and ran his finger between the overlapping fabric. She backed up, her knees hitting the seat of the chair. She sidled away.

"Afraid of me, Norris?" he taunted gently.

She licked her lips. If she told him the truth, that she was more afraid of her response, her need for him, she'd have no defenses left.

He took a step to the side, standing in front of her, crowding her. "If you want me to go, all you have to do is say so."

She nodded and opened her mouth to tell him to leave. "No."

He grinned, a fierce, feral grin that wiped her out. "Drop the robe."

Suddenly, the robe slithered to the floor. Norris glanced down, surprised to see it there. She raised her eyes to Adrian. "Why are you doing this to me?"

He glanced around her living room, selected a chair and sat. He propped one foot over the other knee, a pose she'd seen so often. He looked familiar, somehow comforting, yet out of place. He ran his hand over his chin. The slight rasp of his stubble grated down her spine.

"There have been some changes since you left," he said conversationally, as if she wasn't standing nude before him waiting for him to tell her why he was there.

She said nothing.

"Personnel changes. Policy changes." He waited, as if expecting her to ask for details. She kept her mouth firmly closed.

He nodded, as if he understood her refusal to give him the satisfaction of her curiosity. "For one thing, all programs are now strictly exercise and diet." He paused. "The same thing you'd find at any spa," he added with a dismissive gesture.

That got her goat. "Afraid I'd tell the authorities?"

He had the gall to laugh. "No. Afraid we'd have too many applications."

She rolled her eyes. "Sure. You'd have women coming out of the woodwork to be abused."

He studied her. "You really are an innocent, aren't you?"

"Not anymore," she retorted.

"Ah, Norris. You have no idea." He eyed her, making her wonder.

"About what?"

"There are people who get off on being dominated. Abused, as you put it."

"Not me!"

"Really?" He lifted an eyebrow. "How do you explain how you felt and acted when you were under my control?"

"Not by choice."

"Answer me." His voice was cold and firm again.

She didn't want to tell him a thing. Didn't want to admit that once she'd submitted and accepted his control, she'd felt comforted. Protected. Cared for. Possessed and yet free. Free to experience anything and everything.

"Would you like to feel that again?" he asked softly.

How could he read her so completely? She turned her back on him, afraid to let him see her face, see her nipples, the way they'd pebbled.

He came to stand behind her. Close but not touching her. "Normally, after clients are released from the program, I go on to the next without a thought. I see them if they come back for a refresher course, but they don't stick in my mind."

She felt his heat envelop her. His forest-clean scent claimed her senses. Without touching her, he surrounded her with himself.

"But not you. I can't stop thinking about you."

It would be so easy to lean back and rest against his broad chest. It would feel so good to have his arms around her again, to have him play with her body and satisfy all her senses. It would be so easy to slip back into her old habit of submitting to his will.

Instead, she held herself very straight, fighting him and her own needs with all her will. "You have a strange way of showing it. You didn't even say goodbye."

"That was wrong of me." His admission startled her. He'd never admitted to any weakness, any failure. She turned to study his face. His expression was open and smiling. His eyes drew her in with their warmth. "I'm sorry."

She hardened her heart. "You could have answered my phone calls. Even called me yourself. Instead you show up out of the blue expecting me to welcome you with open arms."

"I think of you in my arms. Naked and passionate. I think of you fighting me, refusing to give in. I think of you coming apart for me. I want you, Norris."

She shuddered, heat surging through her veins. It exploded against her spine, ricocheted back along her ribs and grabbed her heart.

"What if I don't want you?" she whispered. "After all, we have nothing in common."

"Don't we?" he asked softly.

"I like meat," she gasped, trying to resist the need spiraling through her. "I don't like exercise!"

"I sold my partnership in *Sweet Discipline*," he murmured, so close she felt his warm, moist breath on her ear, but still he didn't touch her. "I'm no longer a trainer."

She felt her mouth drop. She turned on her heel. "You owned it?" She glared at him. "*You* were taking my money to treat me that way?" She stomped her bare foot. "I was paying *you*?"

He blinked. "What's the difference? You paid the fees. You knew I worked there. Didn't you think I got paid for what I did?"

"I was paying you for sex?" she screeched.

His mouth opened then shut. He glared at her. "You don't think much of me."

She hurt, she hurt so bad. Here she'd almost believed she'd fallen for him, not just sexually, but as a man who could complement her life. A man she wanted all the days of her life. And then she found out that he hadn't been just an employee at *Sweet Discipline*, but an owner! The knowledge left her reeling.

"Why did you sell?" she asked when she'd won her battle for control.

He shrugged. "It didn't satisfy me anymore."

"I can see why not," she sneered. "Once you changed the policy and stopped forcing women to submit to you, I understand why all the fun went out of your games."

"Believe what you want. But you were the only one."

"Oh sure. That's why it's called *Sweet Discipline*." She rolled her eyes. "Who named it that anyway?"

"I did. A private joke."

She gaped at him. "You expect me to believe I'm the only woman you ever treated that way? You got so good at what you were doing the first time around?"

"Woman, no. Client, yes." He hesitated. His mouth firmed. "I'm a dominant. I've had experience."

All the breath whooshed out of her lungs. "You have some nerve! First you've never done it before and now you have experience?"

"I said you were the only client. My personal life was my own. Until I met you."

She sank down on the couch. "Let me get this straight. You make women submit to you?"

He sighed. "Okay. Listen up." He eyed her until she sat quietly. "As a part owner and trainer I helped clients meet their goals of weight loss. I didn't have sex with them. Only with you."

"Why me?"

He held up his hand for silence. "I told you. I needed a challenge. At work, in my personal life. I kept everything simple at work. No personal involvement with any client. For sure, no sex."

"What about all those sex toys?" she demanded. "I definitely remember you saying you didn't give them to clients so early in their stay. That means sex to me."

He shrugged. "Many of our clients are women with active sex lives. Going six weeks without sexual release would be a hardship. *Sweet Discipline* caters to all a client's needs."

Norris rolled her eyes. "Oh sure, you provide butt plugs for all."

"That was my personal contribution."

"Why?"

"Something you need to understand. On my own time, my personal relationships with women were different."

"Were?" she questioned quickly.

"Were," he said. Firmly.

"So how were they different?"

"I told you. I'm a dominant. I had submissive women."

"You did all those things to them?" It was hard to breathe. "The ropes? The...the..."

"Dildos? Those and more."

Her eyes felt three miles wide. He answered her next question without her asking.

"A submissive woman belongs to her dominant partner. She gives herself to him. Her body is his to do with as he pleases." He kept her gaze. "Sometimes he has to train her to his needs and that can be hard." He paused, as if making sure he had her full attention. "In return for the gift of her submission, a dominant has certain responsibilities."

"Like what? Keeping the handcuffs shiny?"

His grin was there and gone in an instant. "No. He protects his submissive. Keeps her from harm. If he loves her, he cherishes her above all others. He takes very good care of his possession. *I* take very good care of my possessions."

Cherish? Love? Those were words she never associated with Adrian. Hearing him reveal a tender side along with his masculine possessiveness made her realize how much more she wanted from him. "You were training me to be your...whatchallit?"

"My submissive?"

She nodded.

"Yes."

That one word. So simple. So clear and cold. Just *yes.*

"Without my knowledge?"

"Yes."

"But why?" she got out. She cleared her throat. "Why me?"

"I wanted you. Wanted to see if it might become mutual."

"But what if I didn't want you? What if all that was for nothing?"

His mouth hardened. "Then I'd have let you go."

"But you did let me go," she reminded him.

He nodded.

"Why did you do that?" She didn't try to hide the hurt in her voice.

"It was hard," he admitted. "I didn't want to but I wasn't sure your submission then wasn't based only on sex. I had to know how you'd do once you left the spa. If you'd still want me."

"I was miserable," she admitted in turn.

"I know. I kept an eye on you. I thought I'd have to pummel that guy with you tonight."

She fought back a grin at the idea of Adrian walloping on Jack. Mess up that perfect look, then something he'd said registered. She frowned. "You said you'd seen me. When?"

"Before you registered. After we got your application."

She'd known they researched their clients, but this was more. Different. Threatening. She felt stripped, exposed, much more than just being naked in front of him. "You checked me out?" Swallowed hard. "Spied on me?"

"You could call it that." He nodded. "I needed to know more about you."

"So what did you do? Pick my name out of a hat and say this one?" She gestured, her hand pointing at a nonexistent person. "That one will do?"

He laughed. "Hardly."

"Why me, Adrian? Why me?"

"I told you. I saw you. I liked what I saw."

She blew him a raspberry. "You expect me to believe that? You saw me overweight and had the hots for me? Right."

"Strangely, I didn't care about your weight. I liked you, the person. I liked your spirit, your generous heart, even your stubbornness." He smiled at her, slowly, tenderly. "I like you even better now."

"Yeah, right," she scoffed. "You tried to break me down, to change me—and you tell me you liked the old me?"

"More than liked. You fascinated me. You still do."

"Strange way of showing it! Tethering me to that bar, making me kneel to you, making me ask permission to speak!"

"I had to make you learn control. Want something bad enough to fight for it."

"I could have done that without being humiliated."

"Could you? Would you have learned to trust your body, to control your reactions and your desires?"

She didn't answer him.

"Would you have learned how to prolong your sexual pleasures? Would you have given yourself to me so completely?"

She turned away. The memories of those heat-filled nights with Adrian made her too susceptible to him now.

"I wanted you then, Norris. I want you now." He came to her, standing so close she felt the heat of his body though he didn't touch her. "I had to find out if you were strong enough, sure enough of yourself to learn submission. If you were strong enough to be my submissive partner."

"You mean weak and humble, don't you?"

He shook his head. "A true submissive has to be strong to know what she's doing. She has to trust her dominant partner to take care of her in all things. And with that trust, the Dom can't fail her." He touched her then, a slow caress along her jawline. "I didn't fail you when you were my client. I won't fail you now."

Her heart did flip-flops. No way. She wasn't going to fall for this. "I don't believe you."

"That's your choice."

"I don't know you. I don't even know your last name."

"You know me well enough. The rest will come. And it's Townsend."

Adrian Townsend. It sounded right.

She didn't know what to make of him. He was always so sure of himself, so certain, as if he knew all there was to know about her. Did he expect her now to fall to her feet and submit to him again? Her breathing changed with the thought. She needed to think. She hardened her heart. "I want you leave."

He studied her for a moment. Nodded, and went to the door. He opened it, then looked back at her. He studied her for a moment, then without a word, left.

Her heart slowed into a steady, painful beat. He'd answered her questions, raised others and left her bleeding, mourning him.

Chapter Fourteen

She dragged herself to work the next day, and then the day after that and all the days following, feeling like half a person. Not just physically smaller, but as if her heart had somehow shrunk along with her body, leaving her able to feel only grief.

She kept telling herself she'd done the right thing sending Adrian away. Adrian with his claims to want her for herself even before she'd dropped all those extra pounds. How could he lie like that to her?

Jack Rodriguez asked her out again. She refused him, just as she refused other men who gave her svelte new figure an appreciative once over and came back for a second, longer look.

"What's with you?" Kendra shook her head over lunch one day. "You lost the weight. You're skinny and gorgeous and sexy, and you're telling all these guys no?" She narrowed her eyes. "Are you nuts?"

Norris shrugged. "They don't interest me."

"I don't understand you. You've got it. You're flaunting it. Who are you saving it for?"

Good question. The only man she wanted to get naked with was Adrian and she'd blown that. Even if she went back nude, crawling, begging for another chance, he'd probably laugh at her.

Even if she wanted to, where would she find him?

And then, as if he'd heard her question, he left a message on her machine. "If you've been missing me as much as I've been missing you, meet me." He named the date and time and gave her the room number of a well-known hotel. "The key will be at the desk."

Why a hotel? Why a room? He knew where she lived. Why someplace anonymous? Why couldn't they meet for lunch, dinner or even a drink? Why a hotel room?

Hotel rooms had beds. But so did her apartment. So did he, wherever he lived. But never mind the logistics. He'd called her!

Her pulse picked up. Heat flowed through her. She lived in a constant flush until she picked up the hotel key a few minutes before the arranged time.

The room was quietly opulent. Fresh flowers and champagne in an ice bucket rested on a table. A large bed and sitting area took up most of the space, draped windows overlooked the park below and the cityscape. She gave it all a passing glance, checked her watch and quickly, feverishly, undressed.

She hung up her clothes on cedar hangers, and dropped to her knees in the middle of the carpeted floor. She'd had a full body massage, a pedicure and manicure, and carefully shaved, just the way he liked her, bare and extra-sensitive. She waited in her submissive pose, getting more anxious by the moment, until she heard the door open, then close. The lock clicked into place.

She dropped her head and opened her palms on her thighs, not looking up even as the tips of black shoes almost touched her knees.

"Very good, Norris." His voice, dark, severe and yet tender, satisfied.

She kept the position.

A black carryon bag came into her view as he deposited it on the floor. "Stand."

Without another word, she rose lithely to her feet. She pressed her lips to his throat and silently began to undress him.

She peeled back his jacket, slipped it off him and hung it next to her clothing in the closet. Carefully, methodically, she took one item of clothing after another from his well-toned body and disposed of it neatly. He lifted one foot, then the other, as she dropped again to her knees and removed his shoes and socks.

She bent her head and put her mouth on his bare foot. Kissed him.

He sighed as he accepted her submission. Grasping her shoulders, he lifted her to her feet, then turning her, flung her to the bed.

She landed face down, half off the bed. Her breath whooshed out as her head bounced on the mattress. She wasn't hurt, but astonished.

"Don't move."

She remained where she was, peeking at him from the corner of one eye.

"There are some things we have to get straight, Norris."

She nodded, her nose rubbing against the silken coverlet.

"You didn't believe me when I went to your apartment. That angered me."

She swallowed. "I'm sorry."

"I accept your apology."

She relaxed, grateful that it had been so easy.

"You still have to make up for it."

She tensed. There was no bar here, nothing to truss her up, but she knew he'd discipline her.

"Do you understand what I want?"

"My submission."

"Totally and completely," he confirmed. "Are you ready to give me that?"

"I'm here, aren't I?"

"That's not good enough. Are you willing to prove it?"

What more could she do? She was here, naked. She'd positioned herself, kissed his foot in submission, was ready for him. What more did he want?

As if he read her mind, he ran his hand over her butt cheeks. "Such a pretty ass. Toned and tight. I spread you, didn't I?"

She licked her lips. Nodded.

"I gave you pain and then pleasure, didn't I?"

She nodded again.

"The pain enhanced the pleasure?"

She swallowed, remembering. Her breasts felt fuller, tighter. Her pussy opened and went wet. "Yes," she whispered.

"How much more can you take, Norris?"

"I don't know," she admitted hesitantly.

"Shall we find out?"

She cleared her throat. "How?"

"Part of being my submissive means taking as much discipline as I want to give you. It means taking it for me.

To please me. Or to correct you when you displease me." He paused and stroked between her butt cheeks, rimming her anus with a fingertip. "Can you take pain for me?"

She remembered the dildos and the leather sleeves. "I already have."

"Some," he acknowledged. "Can you accept my mark?"

Her heart fluttered within her chest as he continued, "Take my mark on your ass? Take the pain without a sound?"

"Do I have to?"

"No. It's your choice." He stepped back. "I'll give you a moment to decide whether you want to belong to me completely, without reservation, or walk out of here untouched."

Her anus felt cold without his touch. She scrambled upright on the bed and watched him as he made himself comfortable in an easy chair. He turned his head to look out the window, giving her a moment's privacy.

He asked much. She wanted him, wanted him desperately, wanted his possession, his care and protection. Above all, she wanted his love. He hadn't said the words, but why else would he be here if he wasn't ready to commit himself to a loving relationship? That commitment came with such a high price. Could she pay it? Could she meet his standards? And pain, oh, could she take any more? If she agreed, she'd have no choice and one but herself to blame if the pain proved too much. If she put on her clothes and walked out of here, she knew it would be the last time she'd ever see him.

It was cruel. Emotional blackmail. Manipulation. It could also be heart-stopping pleasure, a sense of completion and belonging she'd never experienced before. It was also freedom to experience every bit of pleasure her body—and his—was capable of.

Could she do it? Could she take whatever pain he gave her in return for the pleasure he gave her? And allowed her to give him?

Heart fluttering, she studied his profile. Stark, severe, uncompromising. He demanded much from her. He also gave her much. He understood her, appreciated her, wanted her. That knowledge was heady, undeniable. She took a deep breath. "Yes."

He turned to face her. "You understand there's no going back?"

"Yes."

"Do you trust me?"

She thought of the times she'd handed control of her body to him. How he'd taken her from an obstinate and temperamental woman with no self-control to a woman who believed in herself. "I trust you."

"One last time. Will you take my mark?"

She swallowed. "I want it."

"Good." He rose to his feet, naked, totally at ease, masculine and potent. His erection made her mouth water. "Let's put your acceptance to the test."

She remained where she was while he retrieved his carryon and unzipped it. He looked at her. "Turn down the bed."

She hopped off it, and pulled the coverlet and blankets back, folding them neatly at the end. He nodded approval. "On your belly. In the middle," he corrected when she lay down on one side. "Can you reach each side of the mattress?"

"Yes," she mumbled against the sheet as she touched the sides.

"This isn't the right equipment for this, so we have to improvise." He repositioned her, pulling her down so that her knees came off the edge of the bed and rested on the floor. She wound up kneeling, bent forward over the bed. "Whatever I do, don't move. Don't make a sound. If you need a gag, I'll give you one." He bent over, turning her head to look at him. "Understand?"

She looked into his eyes, saw the emotions he usually kept hidden, and trusting him, nodded.

"Very good." He reached behind him and pulled out a slender rod from his bag. Her eyes widened as she understood what he meant to do. She flicked a glance up at him, saw the set look to his face and buried hers in the covers. Her muscles tensed as she waited for the blow.

Instead of the rap she expected, Adrian ran the tip of the rod along her spine from her nape to the furrow between her cheeks. She shuddered at the almost-caress, her muscles easing, then relaxing further as he stroked the rod along her thighs and calves. He slid it between her legs, gently caressing her pussy as he rubbed it along her bare flesh. The light tap on her clit made her squirm. She felt herself grow moist.

The blow, when it came, was totally unexpected. Light, stinging, it slashed the top of her thighs. She flinched and cried out.

"No noise," he reminded her with the next stroke.

She grabbed a handful of fleece blanket and stuffed it in her mouth.

He hit her again. "That's three. Can you take ten, Norris?"

Oh no, she'd never last, never be able to sit again! She pulled the fleece from her mouth, gasping for air. She meant to beg him to stop, but instead, her pride made her say, "For you, yes."

"Very good, Norris." The next blow fell on her ass, followed by two more. "Count."

Whack! "Seven."

Slash! "Eight," she wheezed.

She heard the rod, tensed, and bore the pain. "Nine!"

Only one more, she thought through a haze of heat. This one, lower, cutting between ass and thigh, hurt more than the others. She moaned, swallowing the pain, and whispered, "Ten."

Adrian dropped the rod on the bed. He sank to his knees behind her and kissed her stinging butt. "You did well," he murmured, "for a novice. We'll keep at it until you're capable of more."

She breathed hard. More? She ached all over, not just her thighs and ass. Her arms hurt and her fingers were numb from hanging on to the bed. Her lips were sore where she'd bitten them, and he wanted her to take more? In a haze of hurt, she didn't at first realize that his caresses on her ass had left her burning inside. Wanting, empty and moist. Becoming aware of her desire, she felt something cool, recognized it as the lubrication he used to ease anal penetration. Oh, not there, not when she hurt so much already!

He ignored her protest, taking a moment to cover himself with the lube, then he knelt and grasped her hips and began to push his prick into her. She tensed, groaning, and stopped when he slapped her flesh below the hip.

"Relax," he ordered sternly. "You can take me."

"But I'm hurting," she protested.

"Take the pain for me, Norris." He reached between them, between her cheeks and stroked her pussy lips. She realized how wet she was, how eager for him to push his finger, his cock, something, into her to relieve the aching need.

He played with her clit, stroking, pulling, and pinching it until she shivered with desire. "Do you want me?" he whispered in her ear.

"Come in me, please." She could barely get the words out.

He pinched her clit. "When I say, Norris, not before."

She whimpered.

He shoved a finger, then two, into her. It was good, but not enough. She wanted more, but held her tongue.

Stroking her ass, fucking her with his fingers, he fondled her higher and higher into a near-mindless state. He pushed into her from behind, an inch at a time, grunting with pleasure as he seated himself deeply in her ass.

Norris shuddered with pleasure. Adrian was in control; he possessed her body, knew its capabilities and pushed her, shoved, and coaxed her into more. Pleasure spiraled through her veins, grabbed at her insides and made her dizzy.

Adrian withdrew, slammed into her, withdrew and slammed again and again. His balls caressed her with each stroke. She felt him deep, deeper than ever before, claiming her, owning her. She relished the sensations, pushed her bottom back and up so he could take her harder, and thrilled to the hard, singeing heat of him. "Ah..."

"Don't come yet, Norris. Not until I give you permission." Adrian's voice was rough, his breathing harsh.

"I'll try," she gasped.

"Don't try. Just do it!"

He pumped in and out, flicked her clit, bent over and bit her shoulder and she took it, took it all and craved more, wanted everything he wanted.

His breathing changed, his strokes becoming fiercer. She felt his balls contract and waited, waited.

At last, he shuddered. "Now," he commanded. "Come now!"

At last! She convulsed under him, shaking with her release, her internal muscles grabbing at his fingers, gripping his cock. She came so hard, so good, so long. And still felt him plunging into her, prolonging her orgasm until she feared she'd pass out.

He came in a great gush, sending his heated sperm high into her ass. She felt it coating her insides, easing his withdrawal as he collapsed behind her, his body heavy on hers. His breath was hot and moist against her neck.

She panted, struggling for breath, while her body slowly regained awareness. She hurt from her head to her toes digging into the carpet. Adrian was still leaning on her, his weight pushing her into more discomfort. She twitched a shoulder.

He grunted, but lifted himself high enough that she could scoot out from under him. She dropped to the carpet, curling into herself, trying not to moan. It seemed ages before Adrian roused, then he got to his feet and went into the bathroom. She heard water running, then he was back, reaching for her, helping her to her feet. With his help, she stumbled into the bathroom and stepped into the tub, yelping when her bruised bottom touched the hot water.

He eased her into it, murmuring softly as he kissed her forehead. "Easy does it." He pushed her gently into the water until it covered her breasts.

Her back, buttocks and thighs stung fiercely, then as the heat of the water eased tense muscles, she relaxed and the pain lessened. She leaned back against the tub and let the water work its magic. She heard water running into the sink and the sounds he made as he washed his cock. The water stopped. She felt him cross the bathroom. With her eyes closed, she couldn't see, didn't want to see his face, but she felt his fingers caress her arm, then lift her hand to his mouth. He pressed kisses to each of her knuckles. "You did well, Norris. I'm proud of you."

She opened her eyes. "Was that necessary? You know I want you. You didn't have to hurt me to prove it."

He said nothing, only looked at her, letting her see his eyes. She gazed deeply, wondering how he could act and look so tender, yet hurt her without a qualm. How could he say he wanted her and yet inflict pain? "I don't understand," she whispered.

"You will." He took her hands and lifted her out of the water. Allowing her to do nothing, he dried her, then rubbed salve into her welts. He touched her gently, carefully, with assurance, knowing just how to ease her lingering pain. She stood quietly, turning this way and that as he wanted, taking comfort from him as she'd taken the hurt.

He capped the tube of salve and placed it on the counter. Taking her into his arms, he held her close. "Come to bed."

She leaned back enough to see his face, see the tenderness there. Her stance pushed her belly forward, pressing it against his engorged penis. Her eyes widened. How could he be aroused again, so soon?

He smiled and led her from the bathroom to stand beside the bed while he straightened the covers. He lowered her to the mattress and covered her body with his. Where before he had caused her pain, arousing her through pain, now he aroused her with gentleness. He kissed and stroked her body, forgetting none of her extra-sensitive places, kissing the welts on her ass and thighs. He licked and nibbled, making her forget everything but the touch of his mouth, lips and tongue and the caress of his hands. He nuzzled her breasts, then sucked on them, gently at first, then increasingly harder until her nipples pebbled and hardened.

With his body, he worshiped her. With his words, he assured her. And when he entered her at last, when she was beyond ready and crying for his touch, he claimed her. Mastered her with compassion and confidence. Cherished her. They came together in a long, slow orgasm that lost nothing for being leisurely yet heartrending. She cried from the beauty of the shared intensity. He cuddled her, letting her tears singe his skin, while he stroked her back. At last, she blinked away the last tear. "I'm all right, now."

They lay entwined together, their bodies gradually cooling. He watched her, his eyes searching hers for a long moment. Apparently finding what he sought, he spoke. "You're willing to be my submissive?"

She nodded.

"Willing to accept me as your dominant partner?"

She nodded yet again.

"Tell me."

"I missed you, Adrian. I want you. I need you."

"There's more. Tell me."

She sighed. Somehow she knew that she would be the first to speak the words. "I love you."

He nodded. His eyes closed, a smile of satisfaction softening his hard features.

"Well?" she prompted.

He asked a question of his own. "Do you know what I expect of you?"

"I'm sure you'll tell me."

Grinning at her sarcastic tone, he propped himself up on one elbow to look into her face. His features changed, becoming serious and severe. "You'll move in with me. You will be naked at all times with me. You will serve me in every way, any way I want, whenever I want. Your body will be mine to do with as I wish. You will belong to me alone."

She gulped.

"If you need discipline, I will apply it. If I want to hurt you to bring you greater pleasure, I will. I will be your master. When you are with me, your only objective will be to satisfy me."

She placed her finger against her lips. When he nodded, giving her permission to speak, she asked, "What about my work?"

"You will continue to do the best you can. You will work whatever hours are necessary; do what is required to grow your business. I will support you however I can. You will take pride in your accomplishments. That is your public side. I will also have a public persona."

She nodded.

"Your private side belongs to me. I will decide where we go, what we do, who we see. You give up all choices to me."

She looked back at him, accepting but not yet sure.

"In return, I will protect you. Treasure you. Trust you. Comfort you when you need it. I will fill your every need. Satisfy your body, keep you warm and secure. I will take no others, be faithful to you as you are to me."

She sighed. Her smile started small but she could feel it grow as happiness bloomed within her. "I will. But…"

He frowned.

"I need the words, too."

His frown disappeared. "Didn't I just tell you? I want you, Norris, not just in bed but all the time. I love you. I want you to be my submissive, my lover, my wife."

"Yes." She pulled him down until he covered her with his body. There was no pain, no doubt. She felt him along the length of hers, hard, heavy and hot. He filled her world. He was her world. She touched her tongue to his throat, tasted his salt. Absorbed him with all her senses.

"Then you give your trust to me? Belong to me?" he asked. "Accept my discipline?"

"Discipline can be very sweet," she murmured and took him into her body and her heart.

THE END

About the author:

A degreed historian, Bonnie Hamre puts her travels in the US, South America and Europe to good use in her novels. Multi-published in contemporary and historical fiction, Bonnie has recently moved to the Northwest, where new adventures await her.

Bonnie welcomes mail from readers. You can write to her c/o Ellora's Cave Publishing at 1056 Home Avenue, Akron OH 44310-3502.

Why an electronic book?

We live in the Information Age—an exciting time in the history of human civilization in which technology rules supreme and continues to progress in leaps and bounds every minute of every hour of every day. For a multitude of reasons, more and more avid literary fans are opting to purchase e-books instead of paperbacks. The question to those not yet initiated to the world of electronic reading is simply: *why?*

1. *Price.* An electronic title at Ellora's Cave Publishing and Cerridwen Press runs anywhere from 40-75% less than the cover price of the <u>exact same title</u> in paperback format. Why? Cold mathematics. It is less expensive to publish an e-book than it is to publish a paperback, so the savings are passed along to the consumer.

2. *Space.* Running out of room to house your paperback books? That is one worry you will never have with electronic novels. For a low one-time cost, you can purchase a handheld computer designed specifically for e-reading purposes. Many e-readers are larger than the average handheld, giving you plenty of screen room. Better yet, hundreds of titles can be stored within your new library—a single microchip. (Please note that Ellora's Cave and Cerridwen Press does not endorse any specific brands. You can check our website at www.ellorascave.com or

www.cerridwenpress.com for customer recommendations we make available to new consumers.)

3. *Mobility.* Because your new library now consists of only a microchip, your entire cache of books can be taken with you wherever you go.

4. *Personal preferences are accounted for.* Are the words you are currently reading too small? Too large? Too...**ANNOYING**? Paperback books cannot be modified according to personal preferences, but e-books can.

5. *Instant gratification.* Is it the middle of the night and all the bookstores are closed? Are you tired of waiting days—sometimes weeks—for online and offline bookstores to ship the novels you bought? Ellora's Cave Publishing sells instantaneous downloads 24 hours a day, 7 days a week, 365 days a year. Our e-book delivery system is 100% automated, meaning your order is filled as soon as you pay for it.

Those are a few of the top reasons why electronic novels are displacing paperbacks for many an avid reader. As always, Ellora's Cave and Cerridwen Press welcomes your questions and comments. We invite you to email us at service@ellorascave.com, service@cerridwenpress.com or write to us directly at: 1056 Home Ave. Akron OH 44310-3502.

erridwen, the Celtic Goddess of wisdom, was the muse who brought inspiration to storytellers and those in the creative arts. Cerridwen Press encompasses the best and most innovative stories in all genres of today's fiction. Visit our site and discover the newest titles by talented authors who still get inspired - much like the ancient storytellers did, once upon a time.

Cerridwen Press

www.cerridwenpress.com

THE
☥ ELLORA'S CAVE ☥
LIBRARY

Stay up to date with Ellora's Cave Titles in
Print with our Quarterly Catalog.

To recieve a catalog,
send an email with your name
and mailing address to:

CATALOG@ELLORASCAVE.COM
or send a letter or postcard
with your mailing address to:

CATALOG REQUEST
c/o Ellora's Cave Publishing, Inc.
1056 Home Avenue
Akron, Ohio 44310-3502

Discover for yourself why readers can't get enough of the multiple award-winning publisher Ellora's Cave. Whether you prefer e-books or paperbacks, be sure to visit EC on the web at www.ellorascave.com for an erotic reading experience that will leave you breathless.

www.ellorascave.com

Printed in the United States
93686LV00001B/232-261/A

9 781419 952630